ESCAPE TO SUNSET

Sunset SEALs Book 4

SHARON HAMILTON

SHARON HAMILTON'S BOOK LIST

SEAL BROTHERHOOD BOOKS

SEAL BROTHERHOOD SERIES
Accidental SEAL Book 1
Fallen SEAL Legacy Book 2
SEAL Under Covers Book 3
SEAL The Deal Book 4
Cruisin' For A SEAL Book 5
SEAL My Destiny Book 6
SEAL of My Heart Book 7
Fredo's Dream Book 8
SEAL My Love Book 9
SEAL Encounter Prequel to Book 1
SEAL Endeavor Prequel to Book 2
Ultimate SEAL Collection Vol. 1 Books 1-4 /2 Prequels
Ultimate SEAL Collection Vol. 2 Books 5-7

SEAL BROTHERHOOD LEGACY SERIES
Watery Grave Book 1
Honor The Fallen Book 2
Grave Injustice Book 3
Deal With The Devil Book 4

BAD BOYS OF SEAL TEAM 3 SERIES
SEAL's Promise Book 1
SEAL My Home Book 2
SEAL's Code Book 3
Big Bad Boys Bundle Books 1-3

Sunset SEALs Duet #2

LOVE VIXEN
Bone Frog Love

SHADOW SEALS
Shadow of the Heart
Shadow Warrior

SILVER SEALS SERIES
SEAL Love's Legacy

SLEEPER SEALS SERIES
Bachelor SEAL

STAND ALONE BOOKS & SERIES
SEAL's Goal: The Beautiful Game
Nashville SEAL: Jameson
True Blue SEALS Zak
Paradise: In Search of Love
Love Me Tender, Love You Hard

NOVELLAS
SEAL You In My Dreams Magnolias and Moonshine

PARANORMALS

GOLDEN VAMPIRES OF TUSCANY SERIES
Honeymoon Bite Book 1
Mortal Bite Book 2
Christmas Bite Book 3
Midnight Bite Book 4

THE GUARDIANS
Heavenly Lover Book 1
Underworld Lover Book 2
Underworld Queen Book 3
Redemption Book 4

FALL FROM GRACE SERIES
Gideon: Heavenly Fall

NOVELLAS
SEAL Of Time Trident Legacy

All of Sharon's books are available on Audible,
narrated by the talented J.D. Hart.

ABOUT THE BOOK

Navy SEAL Jason Kealoha comes to Sunset Beach to release the ashes of his SEAL brother, who was killed in an attack in Nigeria. A Pacific Islander by lineage, Jason is unfamiliar with the Gulf Coast shores his buddy grew up playing in as a child. He befriends a beauty one night at sunset, as she roams the surf, skipping shells, lost in her own world.

Kiley Worthington is on the run from a sex trafficking cartel she stumbled upon as an investigative reporter in Portland. She decides hiding out in her sleepy beach hometown in Florida makes sense until she can figure out where she can spend the rest of her life in safety. The one-night stand was nice, but the last thing she needs is a huge tatted overly-protective guy who won't leave her alone. His attitude is all hardboiled, but his lips are warm and seductive. If she's not careful, she may never escape.

But Jason turns out to be the right kind of wrong for Kiley, as her enemies find her. In Jason's arms she finds a true sanctuary, as well as a safe place to hide forever.

AUTHOR'S NOTE

I always dedicate my SEAL Brotherhood books to the brave men and women who defend our shores and keep us safe. Without their sacrifice, and that of their families—because a warrior's fight always includes his or her family—I wouldn't have the freedom and opportunity to make a living writing these stories. They sometimes pay the ultimate price so we can debate, argue, go have coffee with friends, raise our children and see them have children of their own.

One of my favorite tributes to warriors resides on many memorials, including one I saw honoring the fallen of WWII on an island in the Pacific:

> "When you go home
> Tell them of us, and say
> For your tomorrow,
> We gave our today."

These are my stories created out of my own imagination. Anything that is inaccurately portrayed is either my mistake, or done intentionally to disguise something I might have overheard over a beer or in the corner of one of the hangouts along the Coronado Strand.

I support two main charities. Navy SEAL/UDT Museum operates in Ft. Pierce, Florida. Please learn about this wonderful museum, all run by active and former SEALs and their friends and families, and who rely on public support, not that of the U.S. Government. www.navysealmuseum.org

IF YOU GOT ANY CLOSER, YOU WOULD HAVE TO ENLIST

I also support Wounded Warriors, who tirelessly bring together the warrior as well as the family members who are just learning to deal with their soldier's condition and have nowhere to turn. It is a long path to becoming well, but I've seen first-hand what this organization does for its warriors and the families who love them. Please give what your heart tells you is right. If you cannot give, volunteer at one of the many service centers all over the United States. Get involved. Do something meaningful for someone who gave so much of themselves, to families who have paid the price for your freedom. You'll find a family there unlike any other on the planet. www.woundedwarriorproject.org

CHAPTER 1

J ASON KEALOHA STEPPED out of his Hummer. The
sunset was bright orange with purple and grey
streaks across the early evening sky. The blue waters of
the Gulf of Mexico were chummed, darker than he'd
seen in pictures, worried and angry, like his own
insides. He could hear the chants of his ancestors,
especially the white-hairs, older women who pounded
drums and beat their palms on their thighs.

He'd felt this way in full battle gear, stepping out of
a Hummer into some hellhole as death and trouble
lurked. Those voices kept him connected to his ancestors from long ago, giving him encouragement and
reminding him that they held a spot for him if things
should not turn out. Sometimes that made all the
difference. Sometimes it made him settle so he could
hear the voices of the other men on his SEAL team,
follow instructions quickly and clearly, and be that
missing piece of their puzzle, their force for good when

they worked so seamlessly together.

Today, that calling, that rumble left him nervous. He had a mission. He held it between the fingers of his hands, those same fingers that wiped dirt from the face of his dying brother after several of their Team had been taken down in that red clay earth in Nigeria. He whispered things to his buddy that were untrue, that he'd be okay, that he'd make it back to the base and the evacs were on their way. His buddy knew he was speaking the lies you tell a dying man when there is no hope. You don't ask if they're in pain because you want them to focus on your eyes and the lies so you can walk with them home.

The blue urn was fashioned with a Trident, compliments of the Navy, as if a family member wanted this on their fireplace mantle. But his buddy Thomas had no family. There were no parents, no women or children to mourn over his passing. That's why Jason had adopted him as his brother. The bond never stronger than that day Thomas passed into the hands of his ancestors, who would take the Haole boy and love him to eternity, until Jason joined again, and they fished the waters of Heaven together. The kahuna would pray over him and bless his journey, so his uhane, or spirit, could travel into the afterlife and to a time of great joy and celebration. Jason asked them to take care of this peaceful warrior, abandoned at birth, but never in battle.

Jason's spine was straight, his footsteps sure. He held the urn as the valuable treasure it was, as if presenting it to the hungry mouth of the ocean. If Thomas' uhane absorbed into a stray shark or large barracuda or even a dolphin or great whale, so be it. Far better than to rot in the ground somewhere and be eaten by worms, to smell, putrefy, decay, and become something unholy and unclean. Thomas was a warrior. His warrior spirit would live on in the unlimited ocean or inhabit the body of a great animal.

The setting sun stung his eyes, dry from the tears he'd shed in silence and in the privacy of several darkened rooms and spaces. On the plane from California, he had held the urn. He tendered it carefully upon touchdown and set it at the desk of the rental car agency when he picked up his Hummer. The clerk eyed it suspiciously but didn't ask.

That made Jason smile. It was the first time he'd smiled in three days.

The chants got louder the closer he came to the ocean. He'd walked the archway of the wooden bridge leading across the dunes to the beach from the street, the one that had brightly painted arrows labeled Paris, New York, Barbados, Texas, and even San Francisco, pointing right, left, and straight up. He traveled on sure footing through the soft white sand to the harder white-grey sand then the wet sand that was slightly tan in color, the path bathed in the light blue and white gentle surf.

Sister ocean was a gentle lover, covering his toes with the lacy foam of her underskirts without revealing her modest parts.

With a wash, his sandaled feet were bathed in sea water up to his ankles. The women started hitting the drums louder, their voices arching up an octave. Watchers on the right and left stood still as he carried out his mission. Nobody stopped him. Everybody kept still.

The butterflies in his gut began to flutter. He took in a deep breath and released the metal canister top, allowing the salty air of the Florida Gulf to mate with the ashes of his buddy just before he heard the kahuna chant the story of how he would travel to the place of eternal sunshine and love. That was Jason's Christian grandmother's doing. She told him it was a place of eternal sunshine and love because her God was the God of Love.

That was good enough for Jason too.

He raised the urn as a sacrifice to the God of the Sun, reached back, then tossed the grey contents into the ocean. Thomas' cloud of bones and flesh hung in the sky, arched and then dissipated into the air before dropping into the bay.

"Safe travels, Thomas," he mumbled. "I look forward to the fishing, the laughter, and yes, the beautiful women with big breasts that will suckle us both and feed us roast pig!"

He laughed. The villagers in Nigeria where Thomas

had been killed would be horrified with the knowledge they'd feast on pig.

All the more reason to do so, Thomas, my friend. My one true friend. My brother. Life was unkind to you, but I promise to make up for it.

He wanted to send him off with laughter because his grandmother had taught Jason that death was a celebration.

Now that you're gone, I can sing the truth. It's no fuckin' celebration. It's the end of one thing and the beginning of another. I am so sorry we did not do the Haka for you. Make them show you in Heaven. And think of me down below.

The waters completely absorbed the particles.

"I will miss you Haole boy. Now you won't have to wear so much fuckin' bugspray and sunscreen. And the angels in Heaven don't wear panties, I'm told, so pick the prettiest and have at it, please, for me."

Jason put the lid on the metal container, brushed off the ash clinging to it, then set it back out of reach of the surf. He washed his hands in the water, drying them on his khakis. He didn't have to examine the beach to know there were eyes on him that might not have approved of him dumping Thomas into their bay.

So be it.

He didn't want to spoil the serenity of the moment, so he saved the urn without tossing it too, because that would make the tongues wag and might bring the authorities. He held the container to his chest and watched as the sun melted into the horizon. The orange turned into dark purple then grey. The wind kicked up. A few gulls flew past, and a pelican dove into the water right near where part of Thomas had landed. It caught a fish.

"Okay, so maybe you won't be a mighty fish. Maybe you'll be a pelican. Or a baby pelican when she brings this to her nest."

That gave him the second smile of the day.

The old kahuna his father, now dead some twenty years, used to consult, cackled in the distance. Jason could see the old man dance around the room like a bird, making fun of the brave warrior who had died so others could live.

It didn't matter that the whole world didn't know about Thomas' sacrifice. He did. So did the rest of the team on SEAL Team 3.

Jason's heart clinched, squeezing one bloody tear as if it made a fist.

It's delicious to miss someone, he thought. *It enhances the feeling of being alive.*

WHETHER IT WAS the pain of loss or the joy of celebration and communion, the tug, that dull ache in his heart felt exactly the same. If he were a zombie, he used to watch in those old horror films when he was a boy, he would have no heart, no expression, and would feel no pain. But because his pain was big, his heart was big. And that made him happy.

Jason scanned both directions, the orange remnants creeping back out to the dark blue water. He knew why Thomas had enjoyed this beach of his boyhood. He could see him frolic in the waves as a young man, throwing shells, playing with other boys, making sandcastles, like Jason liked to do.

But this wasn't Hawaii. This was the land of Thomas' ancestors. These men and women were perhaps like ones who had invaded the islands, altered the local Polynesian population culture forever, and mated with women, leaving mixed raced keikis behind. In Jason's land, it didn't matter, because Hawaii was stronger and more beautiful than any of the devastation she experienced by any of those who tried to conquer her. She would remain beautiful as the old Hawaiian women were. Their hips would rumble under their bright muumuus. Their full lips would be painted bright fuchsia or red.

Thomas' relatives were sailors—perhaps pirates, misfits or young men looking for adventure in the Florida Everglades—blown off course from the Caribbean or Cuba. They could have been couples fleeing the big cities of the north or the children and grandchildren of spring breakers, snowbirds, vagabonds, or people just wanting to get as far south in the United States as they could go.

Jason always heard the chanting when he watched the sunsets on Kauai. He didn't hear the ukulele music or the slide electric guitars commonly piped in many of the hotel lobbies, airports, and shopping centers.

He heard the drums and the chanting. His family roots ran deep.

His grandfather said they could trace their ancestors back over four hundred years. When asked, his mother wouldn't tell him if this was true. "They were legendary fisherman, canoe-builders, and engineers who liked to use the powers of the ocean to harness speed and balance."

His grandfather found employment after the Second World War, being unable to serve himself. He liked to show off to the American GIs who were stationed there by climbing coconut trees in his bare feet without any equipment.

Thomas had told him about how everyone came out at sunset. He called it sacred time, and Jason agreed. It was a time to reflect on the day, the dying day, and let the fantasy of the future run wild in the waves and travel between stars at night. It was the celebration of the unknown, as one day collapsed into the arms of the night and then the night fell into the arms of the next morning. It was the cycle and circle of life repeated over and over again, like the lapping of the ocean in its most liquid form, eroding the hardness of the rock and sand on the shore.

He inhaled. The early evening mist on his face felt

good. The older couples strolled north and south along the water's edge. The children squeezed out that last bit of play before they had to come inside, running east and west before slipping into well-lit homes for dinner.

Three older gentlemen in flip-flops and swim trunks with pot bellies and well-tanned skin, one sporting a white ponytail, blasted passed him on their balloon tire motorized bicycles. They were easily in their retirement years and yet looked extremely healthy and happy.

Life as it should be.

He came upon a young woman seated on the sand, a blanket pulled around her body. She wore a large floppy straw hat that covered her almost to her shoulders. Most of her face was obscured in the shadow of the wide brim, and her oversized *Jackie Onassis* sunglasses covered up whatever was left of her face. He knew she was young, because she wore pink frosted lipstick.

As he walked past, he looked down on her. She immediately turned her head to face the other direction. Jason continued his walk.

A few yards later, he felt like running, so placed the canister beneath his arm and assumed a gentle jog. He traveled about twenty minutes, and although he wasn't winded, it was awkward running with a big blue jar in his armpit, so he slowed to a walk.

He examined the row of little bungalows and beach shacks that lined up beyond sand dunes rising up to the right. The windows were no longer bathed in orange, and warm yellow-glowing lights brightly twinkled within the walls. Some houses had fire pits in the yard, where family and friends gathered.

He did an about-face and turned back in the opposite direction, jogging again. When he encountered the young woman with the hat, he slowed and then walked several paces past her. Maybe it was his superstition, the way he'd been trained, or was really a skill he had, but he could feel her eyes on his back.

He sat to fully appreciate the darkness descending all around him. One by one, everyone had disappeared from the beach.

Except the girl in the floppy hat.

Headlights from a beach park vehicle downwind shone on her briefly—just enough so he could see the hat shaking. Even her upper torso, in that one flash of a second or two, was vibrating. Her hands moved to her face under the hat. As the light was redirected elsewhere, in the darkness, he heard her sniffle.

She'd been crying.

He stood, working his way over to see if she needed assistance. Before he could reach her, she scrambled to her feet, nearly tripping on the blanket she'd thrown aside, and ran straight for the wooden arched bridge and beach access path leading to the parking lot and the main street beyond, leaving the blanket behind.

And then she disappeared.

CHAPTER 2

KILEY RAN AS fast as her legs would keep her upright. She clutched the oversized hat with her right
hand and in her left, she carried her beach bag, which
now felt like it weighed fifty pounds. She nearly stumbled several times in the soft sand, her balance thrown
off by the dark night. Ripping off the hat, she stuffed it
into the bag and tried to stay on her feet, keeping her
forward momentum. She felt bound by heavy chains
pulling on her body, yanking her down into the abyss
of the ocean. Her feet felt encased in concrete.

They found me!

She didn't dare turn around to see if the hulking
man continued to follow her. That wouldn't be their
style anyway. They would've sent two or three goons
together. A single guy like this could be the lookout
and then they'd come for her later, so she ran until she
hit the wooden bridge, stubbing her big toe on a nail
that popped out. But she kept going, knowing that her

foot was bleeding. At any minute, the floor would collapse and she'd be swallowed up by the earth underneath.

The house she rented was located on the left side, so she abruptly turned right and ran until she came to another access road dead ending at the beach. Just after she rounded the corner, she hid, looking down the narrow alleyway to see if she could discern any movement. There was not much of a moon tonight so her eyesight failed. Movement here and there turned out to be palm fronds or other bushes blowing in the gentle breeze.

Her heart thundered, almost to the point of making her choke with each inhale and exhale. She could hear her breathing inside her head as she stumbled in the dark. Her throat was red hot, starved for moisture, her lips parched and raw from her gasping run.

She was going to have to find some way to defend herself when she ventured out again. The steak knife in her bag wasn't nearly good enough as a weapon.

What was I thinking? Of course they would find me!

Desperate for something safe, a place without fear of being discovered, she had just wanted to get her life back. She was tired of the months of dangerous investigations, the police interviews which went nowhere, and the phone hang ups—all due to the articles she'd written for several Northwest newspapers, including the Columbia Passage. She'd run away to the land of her childhood. It wasn't safe back in Portland any longer. Probably never would be safe there again.

She'd revealed information she obtained from an anonymous source about the sex and drug trafficking trade, which had made her persona non grata in the town she loved. She had a target on her back—prey for the monsters who ran the child exploitation and sex trafficking ring in the Portland area. What started out being something she was deeply committed to, saving young innocent lives, had now turned into something that could very well cost her own life.

Alone, even disconnected from her fellow reporters, she didn't know who she could trust. She wasn't sure she could trust her own editor, who promised to guard all her secrets and her sources. But somehow these had been inadvertently leaked. One of the college interns helping her was killed in an auto accident, and one of the victims she used as a source had disappeared. Could it have been someone on the paper staff or a worker at the coffee houses she frequented? Everyone around her was a suspect.

Her parents had sold their Beach House in Florida five years before. After their failed attempt to relocate to Northern California to be closer to Kiley's brother, they moved to Portland to be part of their daughter's life. She knew her mother was hoping that she'd find a nice young man, settle down, and raise a family. It felt like they moved to Portland just to witness such a happy event.

But that was not to be. A year after their move, both her parents passed.

Her work was taking so much of her time that she even lost touch with her brother, Sam. Now, asking for Sam's help, would only land him in the same kind of trouble Kiley was in. Even though they weren't close, she wouldn't dream or wish this on anyone. She'd decided not to let him in on what she'd uncovered.

Kiley checked her bearings then slipped across the alleyway that separated the first row of beachside cottages with the thicker row of larger homes that bordered Gulf Boulevard. These places occasionally were two and three stories, unlike the bungalows on the gulf side. Smaller shacks were torn down so that huge homes could replace them, all built so they would also have ocean views.

Every dog bark made her jump. Every door that slammed sent her reeling for cover under a tree or beside a fence or hedge.

Gulf Boulevard was busy this time of night, people going to and from dinners or beginning the evening bar hop scene. She could only risk being seen for short periods of time, so she crossed the busy street and entered the subdivision of houses on the canal side of the peninsula. These homes were larger still and away from beach traffic, huge mansions with well-manicured garden areas that would rival a botanical garden. Some of these homes had names affixed the iron gates that kept the occupants safe inside, as if they were huge ocean-going vessels.

She followed the roadway, walking around parked cars and staying in the shadows away from the bright streetlamps occasionally illuminating the area. Sometimes, a car would come from behind, and she would dip inside a gated area as if returning home. Gradually the street veered to the left and ended in a cul-de-sac.

She could see the shivering waters of the canal outstretched behind the large homes. Beyond the canal were lights from a neighboring island, including a strip of beach shops and outdoor restaurants. Music wafted through the night air. She could even smell freshly barbecued seafood.

The cul-de-sac was a dead end for her, so she crossed the street and returned one block then meandered through the subdivision to the first intersection, where she turned. She wandered back-and-forth until she found herself at Gulf Boulevard again but several blocks north of the beach access.

She pushed the button for the pedestrian crossing and quickly traversed Gulf Boulevard, slipping into the first beach access alleyway that appeared. She heard the sounds of people having dinner or gathering outside their houses, enjoying fire pits or having cocktails on the patio.

She kept her eyes peeled for anything that resembled the huge hulking form of the strange man. She'd developed a sixth sense about being followed over the past few months, and tonight was no different, even though she saw no evidence. Her senses were still on high alert and her heart continued racing due to the close encounter.

After winding her way through the driveways and small alleyways connecting various properties to the beach access, she was at last at her front door. Rummaging through her beach bag, she searched for her keys despite the straw hat stuffed tightly there scratching her fingers. She quickly unlocked the front door, closed it quietly so as not to attract attention, and turned the deadbolt, feeling some semblance of safety.

Tossing her beach bag to the side, she heard all the contents scoot over the tiled floor: her cell phone, her lipstick and sunscreen, her book and the serrated kitchen knife she'd put in there for self-defense. She quickly crossed the room and checked the sliding glass door to the sand dunes and ocean beyond, locking it.

At last she began to feel safe. She slumped into her living room couch, propped her feet up, and tried to relax, inhaling long deep breaths through her mouth then exhaling slowly through her nose. She'd been taught this to avoid panic attacks dogging her recently. After several minutes of growing calm, she poured herself a tall glass of ice water, pulled a kitchen chair up to the sliding glass door, and watched for evidence of anyone coming toward her or looking at her from the outside.

She found none.

Kiley thought about what had happened. She'd

been watching the sunset when the big man tossed dust and ashes to the ocean. At first she didn't understand what he was doing, taking him for a homeless crazy tossing sand. But then she realized he had poured—no, thrown—someone's remains into the surf. It was fascinating to watch his muscled shoulder and huge arm pull back and then toss the fragments from the jar he held. Someone nearby had gasped. People stopped talking. Out of the corner of her eye, she saw someone point while others softly chattered like birds on a wire.

Growing up on Sunset Beach, she had never seen this happen before. She thought it was against the law.

But then, he began to run North. Her eyes followed him until he was lost in the crowd of sunset watchers. Several minutes later her reverie was disturbed when he came back, and this time, he slowed down, taking a seat a few yards away from her. Her pulse had raced again as she watched for any further advancement.

She drank her ice water as she continued scanning the beach, still searching for any signs of danger.

Had he sat near her *on purpose*? Had he watched her the same way she watched him, out of the corner of her eye?

After several minutes, her breathing slowed, and her heartbeat returned to near normal. She'd drained her glass of water. It left her chilled.

My blanket!

Her senses, still not returned to normal, began to perk up a tick or two as she squinted, trying to see where she'd left it. She also wondered if the strange man was still there. If he was homeless, he'd most likely be wrapped up in it. Perhaps infesting it with fleas or using it as a place to cover up peeing on himself. She'd brought that blanket all the way from Portland. It was the fuzzy go-to thing she'd always drawn comfort from, nearly as precious as a child's blanket. She couldn't let it become fouled by some berserk behemoth who didn't respect the laws of the beach.

Kiley unlocked the sliding door and stepped out onto her patio. Breathing in the ocean air several times, she felt her soul fill with courage and hope. She was wrapped in her imaginary safety blanket of happy memories from long ago.

The beach heals everything.

The saying had been painted on a plaque on her apartment wall in Portland. It had been in her bedroom growing up, and it followed her to Europe when she did her semester abroad in Paris. It journeyed with her to London and Scotland and throughout Italy as she made her way traveling all summer before the fall semester.

It was the first thing she unpacked when she came back to Sunset.

Carefully, she traversed the soft sand, noticing what appeared to be the discarded blanket off to the left. As she approached, she sniffed but didn't detect an odor. But she discovered that someone had folded the blanket and left it there for her. As she bent to pick it up, a male voice behind her whispered, "I'm glad you came back for it."

She whirled around, clutching the blanket to her chest. She wished she had a knife or a pair of scissors or something to defend herself. But she was going to face this person no matter who he was. She was tired of being so frightened that she could hardly think. She couldn't sleep. She was exhausted from running, hiding.

Before she could get the words out of her mouth or scream for help, he approached her. His huge shoulders and upper torso blocked what little light came from the stars and the crescent moon rising above him. His size and girth registered quickly. She would not be able to fight him off or outrun him.

"Leave me alone!" she yelled.

"Hey, I mean you no harm."

"I said leave me alone, "Kiley reiterated, holding her palm out in front.

"I scared you. I'm sorry I didn't mean to. I apologize. Please, it upsets me to know that I scared you. That's not me."

"Did you not hear me? I want you to leave me alone." She turned to go.

"Wait. Please. Don't be frightened."

She hesitated and then rotated halfway in his direction, still ready to run if she needed to.

"What—what were you doing out here with that…" She pointed to the metal canister barely visible tucked under his arm.

"I came to carry out my best friend's wishes. My buddy lost his life overseas, and I returned him to the sea, to the gulf. This is where he grew up."

She noticed his English had a slight accent she couldn't make out. She corrected her focus.

"I'm sorry. But this isn't a good time for me."

"Nor for me. But please accept my heartfelt apologies for scaring you. It would bother me if you walked away thinking I meant you any ill will or harm."

He didn't sound like a monster or like someone who wanted to take her life. He began to sound like someone she might be able to trust.

That's a ridiculous thought! But before she could fully adjust, she was speaking again to the stranger.

"I've just moved back here. It's been a very difficult few months for me. I…"

What am I saying?

In spite of everything else, her chest tightened. Her breathing became staccato and dangerous. She knew what it was. It was a full-on five-alarm panic attack. At a very inconvenient time.

"I don't feel…"

Just before she lost consciousness, she had expected to hit the hard scratchy sand as her body collapsed, but powerful arms cradled her gently, breaking the fall.

And then everything went black.

CHAPTER 3

JASON HAD NO problem catching the young woman, being especially careful to make sure her head and shoulders didn't come close to hitting the sand. Completely unconscious, her body rolled into his upper torso, which made it easier for him to scoop her up, his right arm placed beneath the backs of her knees. She was light and supple. He judged she was about twenty-five years old.

The blanket he had so carefully folded for her was discarded, lying in a heap at his feet. He didn't want to risk losing his balance and hold her too tight so he didn't retrieve it. He swung her back and forth as if holding a child, rocking and whispering reassurances that she was going to be fine. He caught himself speaking to her in his grandfather's native tongue.

Just as he suspected, within seconds, she began to gain consciousness.

Of course she was confused. It was a lot to take in.

She'd been afraid of him after all, had been fleeing for her life, and now he was holding her, trying to be as tender as he could. He kept his arms out in front, so that as she came to, she wouldn't know how close to his upper body she had been.

"You're going to be okay, miss. You'll be just fine."

"What? Where am I?" she mumbled, stirring in his arms.

"Just take a deep breath in. Keep breathing. That's it. You're gonna feel fine in just a couple of minutes."

At last she realized that he'd been holding her, which caused her to clamor to get to her feet, nearly pushing him aside.

"I told you to leave me alone!" she said as she straightened her clothes.

He couldn't see her face but he was sure she was glaring at him from the sharpness in her voice.

"Okay, okay, take it easy." He stooped, picking up the blanket and shoving it in her direction until her hands could locate it. "Here you go. Take your blanket. Wrap it around yourself so you don't get cold. Are you sure you're okay?"

"Of course I am!" she retorted in a huff.

In the blackness between them, he shook his head and allowed a grin to separate his lips, since she probably couldn't see him anyhow. She was one stubborn and bitter woman, who, unfortunately, still thought he was the enemy. If she only knew.

"What's so funny?" she demanded.

Okay, so much for not being seen.

He allowed himself a chuckle and really didn't care whether she believed him or not. The whole situation was beginning to annoy him. "I've tried just about every way I know how to convince you I mean you absolutely no harm. But if you want to be that way, fine. I don't know what fox got in your hen house but, lady, there's no problem on this end. Now if you don't mind I'm going to get as far away from you, your hat, your blanket, and this beach as possible."

"You have no idea what I've been through," she spat. It stopped his intention to run away.

"How could I? You won't listen to a damn thing I have to say." He let his shoulders fall as he sighed, trying to relax the muscles at the base of his neck. "Look. Let's just call a truce and go our separate ways. Does that meet with your approval, or is there something you don't like about *that* comment?"

His night vision must have kicked in, because he saw her hand flash through the air a millisecond before her open palm slapped him across the cheek. Memories flooded his brain of growing up on the island. Two nasty Samoan sisters in his school who outweighed him by at least three times had bullied him all through grammar school and into Junior High. Until that fateful day he hit one of them back and got expelled.

Reflex made him grab her forearms and yank her into him.

"Stop it, you Haole tart. I won't hurt you but I'll defend myself."

She was wiggling in front of him, trying to keep air space between them. Then she was kicking his shins with her bare feet, hooking herself around his thick legs and trying to get him off balance. Her fingers reached for his face to scratch him, but he could hold both her wrists in one of his hands, the other arm around her waist, immobilizing her the more she tried to struggle.

He stood like granite, gripping her tighter. He gave her absolutely no room to move as he pressed her up against his chest.

"Stop it. You're being a child. I'm not hurting you so just quit."

"I don't quit. I will never quit. I won't quit until you let go of me. I'm going to scream rape if you don't let me go!"

That really pissed him off. He squeezed her wrists together, holding them with just one hand. It made her cry out so he placed his other hand over her mouth. Pressing his nose to her face, he whispered, "Stop it. Dammit. Quit this."

For several long seconds with their noses pressed

against each other, he matched her deep breathing with his own. He assessed her willingness to be reasonable, felt her weakness, and was thankful as she finally stopped fighting him. Her flowery scent made his ears buzz as he allowed her hot breath to wash over his face.

She was strong and determined. Angry and not afraid to fight against an impossible opponent, no matter the danger. She was right. She was not a quitter.

It took another few seconds before she must have determined that there was no real danger present, because just as soon as her fear left, she was shuddering in a series of sobs racking her body. He relaxed his grip on her forearms and folded her into his chest and let her cry against him.

He felt like his hands were too big and clumsy for her delicate neck and shoulders as he brushed up and down her spine, squeezing the top vertebrae until she relaxed further, her shaking now subsiding.

He shielded her from the wind coming from the South, brushed her hair from her face and placed a soft kiss to her forehead. "Don't be afraid. I'm not going to hurt you. I only want to help. Please do not be afraid. I'm here now. Nothing is going to harm you."

Her arm wrapped around his waist, not reaching very far, as she snuggled in the safe space he'd created for her. Jason felt a twinge of regret that he'd been so harsh with her. Her head rested on his chest just below his chin. He ran his fingers through her hair, sifting, whispering things he'd heard as a child when he'd jump into bed at night with his mother after he had nightmares.

Whatever horror movie that had been playing in her head must have been something frightening. He knew what fear smelled like. He'd seen women panic and faint in the path of danger, unable to defend themselves or their loved ones. He'd seen it all too often, and all too often he'd not been able to save them either.

She leaned back, trying to see his face. "What language is that?"

Language?

He must have been chanting, or speaking the circular rhymes they'd sing as kids. It came as second nature, and he couldn't even remember what he'd said.

"Hawaiian. Something my grandmother taught me."

His right palm brushed tentatively against the side of her face, and then he released her all at once and stepped back. His arms fell to his sides.

"I'm sorry. It was a panic attack," she mumbled.

"No, not exactly. The attack was when you passed out. You are scared of something, little one. That was pure, cold fear." He sighed again, wanting to hold her once more, but resisted.

She wrapped the blanket around her.

"Are you in danger?" he asked, suddenly wishing he'd not been so forward.

"A little. But I'm far enough away from all that. Thank you, and I apologize how ridiculous I was."

"No apology necessary. Fear does strange things to people sometimes. But you were brave. You fought well."

"No I didn't. I was pathetic."

"You were difficult to stop. That speaks to your courage, not your skill."

"Did I hurt you?"

Jason let her fingers reach for his cheek which had now turned warm and was probably swollen. She'd packed a good swing and the sting surprised him. He did not back away, allowing the touch. His heart was pounding, beating like the drums of his ancestors as she gracefully twisted her wrist and brushed the backsides of her fingers across the side of his face all the way to his ear.

He could have easily taken her in his arms, and he knew perhaps she'd let him kiss her, but he stood like a statue, feet planted in the sand, like the surfboards standing guard at Hanalei Bay. The wash of waves lapping on the shore stilled his restless and troubled soul, while the distance between their bodies remained. She had the touch of his grandmother and some of the older women of his community—the way she used to bless his cuts and bruises, especially the ones left by the two Samoan sisters.

This stranger was a healer, and yet Jason knew she didn't understand yet what her true capacity was.

AS HE DROVE to his motel room, he knew that, if the Gods of his ancestors wanted him to meet her again, they'd create the opportunity. The empty urn sat next to him on the front seat of his rental Hummer, as if Thomas was witness to this magical connection he felt to her. Maybe Thomas was laughing at him.

He glanced down at the seat.

"We won't speak of it."

The urn obeyed.

But all the way back, he couldn't forget the feel of her shaking body against him, the scent of her hair, the tiny beads of sweat at the sides of her cool forehead, and her probing but gentle fingers.

He thought about her while he showered and then watched moonlight glisten on the water of the Gulf. He thought about her as he lay naked in his bed, his head propped against his forearm.

Jason had left the sliding glass door open a few inches so he could inhale the ocean air all night long, which was always his custom wherever in the world he traveled, if it was safe. He dreamt of the beaches back home, lush and full of the scent of flowers floating all around him. He thought about the tanned Polynesian girls he'd dated and made love to on the beach, their modest nakedness a thing of beauty and grace. He felt their full lips, and the smooth flat of their noses as they cuddled, giggled, and whispered things to him. In those days, drunk on the discovery of sex, he didn't realize how the ocean, the beach and a woman's body could heal all those broken parts he could not.

He thought about the girls he met in Coronado who were a bit too fast for his tastes. They wanted everything now, hard and deep, leaving him aching for a simple touch of kindness or a word of wonder.

Like a metronome, the constant rhythm of the ocean sang him to sleep in stanzas stitched together by the calling of sea birds.

The last thought he had before he drifted off was that Thomas had brought him here to Sunset Beach. It was a bigger purpose than the final goodbyes to his friend. Thomas wanted him to see the place where he'd grown up, to see the beauty and treasure buried here. In time, he'd find out just what that treasure was.

As one door closed, another one was waiting to be discovered. Whatever was on the other side of that door was his destiny.

Tomorrow would be a new adventure.

CHAPTER 4

K ILEY'S NUMBNESS CONTINUED all night long.
She couldn't get warm, even when she put on flannel pajamas—a rarity in Florida. She believed her heart had slowed down so much, all the blood had rushed into her lower body. She shivered in bed, getting up in the middle of the night to take a hot shower. Her body temperature held long enough so she could fall asleep for a few hours. But then she woke up again in the blue light after midnight.

Her dreams were smoky, bright orange and power-ful like the campfires they'd made during college. In Oregon, you could make a beach bonfire if you wanted to. It was considered a form of eco-cleanup, since there were so many pieces of driftwood washing up from the tall trees that had been harvested over centuries all along the coast. She could feel the spirits of the indige-nous peoples, the First Nation, dwelling in the tall trees, looking down on them, waiting.

She hoped it was still the same today, because those trips with friends were the highlight of her college days. They'd sit in circles, gathered like Native Americans, telling stories by campfire, playing music, and drinking beer while the fire crackled and sent sparks up to the sky. Oregon was always damp. Even on bright summer days and early fall afternoons, there was moisture in the air.

Unlike today, she didn't worry then about who might be lurking in the forest or around the barn. Not that it had been safer. Her perception of life had totally changed. She recognized it as a form of PTSD, something her editor teased her about.

She rolled on her side and watched the waves in the moonlight, grateful whomever had designed this little bungalow had thought to put a small window at sleeping-eye level in the bedroom.

She pulled the blanket up to her ears and detected the stranger's manly scent. Kiley remembered the heat of his enormous chest and how his shoulders rose up like mountains of muscle. Nobody looked like that in Oregon, she thought. Not even the football players in college.

She had no idea there were so many evil men and women who preyed on the weak and vulnerable for their own advantage, who had no conscience and would hurt others until someone stopped them. That awareness had taken a long time to fester and grow. It came later, after her parents were both gone, when she experienced what it was like to be truly alone. She was free to go about her life and explore what she wanted to. It was a fair trade to the other darker feelings of loneliness as she pursued her quest for relevance.

It all started one day when Corbin Newman III, her editor, had given a lecture in her English class about writing for the *Columbia Passage*, Oregon's largest paper. He told the story of its long history of righting wrongs, speaking the truth, and searching out knowledge that lay buried, either intentionally or unintentionally. His salt and pepper hair, worn a little too long, curled up at the ends. He also wore round, silver glasses like John Lennon. She never saw him in anything but faded blue jeans and a long-sleeved, button-down shirt, usually rolled up to mid forearms. He had delicate, expressive fingers and hands he liked to use when he spoke. But his eyes were as blue as the water in the Gulf. That was the most shocking thing about him.

He mesmerized the entire class with his stories. He wore suede Birqs with striped socks and wore his wristwatch backwards with the clasp on top of his arm, the dial close to his body. Although married, he never wore a wedding ring, which had been the topic of conversation for several days after he spoke.

Like a moth to the flame, it was rumored that he usually picked two or three young Lewis & Clark girls to do his bidding, calling them interns, but they were much more. Everyone knew he cheated on his wife, and everyone wanted to be one of those girls anyway.

That had been off-putting to Kiley. Maybe that's why Newman fawned so much over her, agreeing to start her out at the paper before she graduated. She talked her way out of impromptu dinners and tried not to be alone with him in the car. Her roommate thought she was completely nuts.

But there was no denying that Corbin Newman III could tell a good story with the reverence and skill of a world-class yarn-teller. He taught them that, if they were going to report the news, they had to make the reader care about the people in the story. Not telling a lie. He wanted them to throw a heavy dose of imagination and fiction, supposition, and mystery into their pieces so someone would look for their byline.

And it worked. Kiley's byline was elevated to the editorial page. Her research on child abuse and women's shelters drew lots of comments on the digital version of the *Passage*. She had a social media following and presence, and she'd been asked to speak at women's conferences and for graduate studies courses.

Kiley wondered why she was even thinking about her editor this evening as she adjusted her body, lying on her back and staring up at the ceiling. She was as far away from that culture and climate as she could be, except for the fact that she was beside a large body of water, the Gulf. In the Pacific Northwest the ocean was angry and churning all the time. So strange that it was called *Pacific,* meaning peaceful. There was nothing peaceful about that ocean or the rugged people who haunted the forests and tolerated the mist and the cold.

She shuddered again, pulled up her covers, and, after battling her racing mind, she finally fell asleep again.

IN THE MORNING, her phone rang, waking her up. The room was bright. With no job to get to, she'd actually slept in until nine o'clock.

Amazing!

"Kiley. You were supposed to call me yesterday. I start wondering when I don't hear from you." Newman sounded slightly annoyed, maybe a little urgency to his voice.

"It got to be late, and—"

"Fuck sake, Kiley. It's three hours earlier there. If it was midnight, and I know you go to bed early, it would only be nine o'clock here. That's acceptable for a phone call."

So she'd gotten caught. "Sorry, Corbin. I was exhausted and nearly passed out."

That part of the excuse was correct.

"You going to get me that story for next Friday? I'm saving a big spot for it, and I have nothing to fill that hole if you don't come through."

"I'll make it. I always do."

"You make me nervous. All this sneaking around."

"We live in a digital age. I can write from anywhere," she informed him. That wasn't the real reason, of course, but it was logical.

"Well, I still think you should check in with the police there, and have them touch base with Portland's finest. You're alone, unprotected."

"What makes you think I'm all alone? I do have certain social skills."

"Oh, that's right. You were a serial dater in Portland. Forgot about that."

The comment hurt. He used to tease her about never getting out of the house, chiding her that there was more life than in the romance books she read every waking second she could. It was of no use trying to explain it to him. She'd rather crawl into a book and live there and would do it in a heartbeat if given the opportunity.

"You worry too much."

"Well, when my lead investigative reporter runs clear across the country because she thinks someone is after her, I do worry. I've got a paper to run. Everything you do in Florida you could do here."

"Except I don't think it's safe."

"Don't you think your imagination is getting the better of you? I mean, we did that story last year about the chief of police in Vancouver. He was related to half the town, and nothing happened when he got fired and then went to prison. Then you write about a women's shelter and supposedly get all sorts of calls..."

"They were real calls, not supposed calls, Corbin."

"Honey, ex-husbands are a dangerous lot, I'll grant you, especially when their wives take off in the middle of the night with their kids. I'm not condoning any of that, but just consider you are over-reacting, won't you? And if not, why don't you get the authorities involved?"

"Because then they'd want my sources, Corbin. You taught me that."

"They might even help your story, give you information about some of these Joes. They could do drive-bys and keep you safe. You know they do that."

"I'm safer here."

"In Florida?" Corbin sighed. "You sure you're not just running off with some beach bum, taking a little vacay in the sun?"

"No, the threats were real. My dead cat was real. My slashed tire was real."

"But you've never been physically accosted. That's

what I'm saying."

"I won't dignify that comment. Corbin, you know a woman has the right to protect herself, and I'm feeling I need protection. Not in Portland. I need some distance for a while."

Whether or not there was anyone after her, she didn't want to tell him she'd had a meltdown at the hands of a stranger, on whose enormous chest she'd unloaded her tears. Finally, she added, "Besides, a couple of goons in leisure suits would stick out like a sore thumb."

"You're blowing smoke up my ass, Kiley. Haven't you ever been to Miami?"

"So what's gotten you so irritable, Svengali?" It was the name all the girls in the dorm had given him. Kiley knew he liked having women throw themselves at him every day. She imagined he would feel virtuous if he didn't partake, and got off on it occasionally.

"We have another missing girl. I would have put you on that case. It could just be an immigration issue or mix up. But this time, she's not fifteen. She's twenty-five."

That did concern her. "What's the story?"

"She's from Ecuador, very small for her age, not even five foot. We're guessing that if she was abducted, like the other victims you discovered, the kidnapper mistook her for a fourteen-year-old girl."

"When did this happen?"

"See, I knew you'd be interested in covering this. But you can't do it from Florida."

"Humor me, Corbin. Just a few of the details."

"It happened the day before yesterday. She was living with a local attorney in town…"

"Who?"

"Miles Benson. Do you know anything about him?"

"Nope. What kind of law does he practice?"

"Well, that's why we think it could be an immigration issue. He is an immigration attorney. Maybe she didn't want any hassle from authorities. Maybe she was unhappy in the household and had no one to turn to. She worked as an *au pair* for the children. But she cooked, cleaned and drove them to all their school things."

"And the attorney called it in?"

"His wife did, yes. According to her, the lady just disappeared."

"Just like the other ones. You know this is connected, Corbin."

"Well, then you're going to love this. She also has long black hair and typically wore it in a ponytail, like many of the other girls."

She thought about it before she replied. "Corbin, I'm still not coming back there."

He sighed over the phone. "I was afraid you'd say

that. I can't say as I blame you. You still have files here. Can I assign them?"

"Go ahead."

"And you'll get me my story in time for Friday, right?"

"Yes, I will." She paused. "Who are you going to put on the story about the missing girl?"

"Martin."

"No, you need a woman on it. The mother has to be interviewed and separately. Are the police involved?"

"Of course they are! This story made headlines this morning."

"Because it's number four."

"According to you, at least number four."

"Yes, probably more like ten." She considered the staff at the paper. "Why don't you put Carmen on it? She speaks Spanish. She can talk to the family of the girl back home."

"Family? According to Mrs. Benson, this girl had no relatives. She was brought up by an agency."

"But she had friends, people Carmen could interview. Nobody's going to trust Martin."

"But he's ten times the reporter, Kiley. Carmen's more interested in the political stuff, the demonstrations, social justice causes."

"Which would be perfect for Martin. He can get in

people's faces. This needs to be handled with delicacy. She'd be talking to people who don't want to tell their story for fear they'll be sent back home. And I like the idea of a woman asking all those personal questions, not a man, Corbin."

"Bingo. Okay, I agree. It's probably an immigration issue. But I'll put Carmen on it for a few days and see if she digs anything up."

"Tell her we can talk via Skype if she wants."

"I'll tell her. Not sure she'll be very thrilled."

"Just because we don't hear about all the suffering that goes on with these women, with children smuggled into the U.S. against their will, doesn't mean it isn't a huge story. Not as juicy as a strike or demonstration. This stuff is more underground, hidden. And it's just plain evil. If my story does what I think it will do, and I have to stay here for a few more weeks, Carmen's going to have all the follow-up. It's a great opportunity for her. With her help, all the little loose ends will be tied up, and we'd have developed a huge case for the police."

"And not something you want?"

"It won't bring back my cat. It won't bring back my peace of mind when I walk out into the dark parking lot downtown. I'm not doing it for recognition. I'm doing it for the women. And right now, with all those stories, I'm too radioactive. Carmen will do a much better job finishing it."

"What about your apartment?"

"Megan's boyfriend is moving in. That was already in the works. I was going to have to move out anyway. I'm just giving her all the furniture and household stuff. She can hold everything else for me until I return."

"So what do I tell people, Kiley?"

"Tell them I'm on a writing retreat. That part is even true."

"And when they ask me where?"

"Tell them Chicago or Cincinnati. Don't mention Florida, please."

"Alright. Now, if you don't get that story in, I'm going to cut back your salary, Kiley. Don't play games with me, okay?"

"This is not a game, Corbin."

"Are you going to give me a forwarding address?"

"Nope. Anything you need to send, you can email to me. My check is on automatic deposit."

"Well, are you having a good time, at least? On the beach somewhere?"

"Don't assume anything. And why would you care?"

"Come on, Kiley, why don't you trust me? Don't you think someone should know where you are?"

"There are people who know where I am."

"Really, who?"

"Look, Corbin, we agreed I was going to disappear for a while. That way when anybody asks you where I am, you don't have to lie."

She checked the time and realized she'd been on the line too long. Somewhere she'd read that anything over three minutes could be traceable, even with a burner cell.

"I'm going to sign off now. I'll call you in a couple of days. You can email me the pictures, and I'll take a look to see if I recognize her, okay? And have Carmen call me if she wants some background information, some of the things I've been working on. There's a new shelter I ran across that I want her to check out"

He gave no objection.

KILEY SHOWERED, MAKING the conscious decision not to open her laptop until she was ready to write. She fixed a light breakfast, made coffee, and walked outside on the sugary white sand beach in front of her bungalow.

This place is worth every penny!

She'd paid double the rental amount to be right on the beach. It wasn't just the view she liked, it was the fact that the constant sound of the water lapping on sand drowned out all the other neighborhood noise and some traffic on Gulf Boulevard. She took the lease for three months and had to pay it up front. It cost nearly what it cost her to live for a whole year in their converted artist's flat in the trendy warehouse district of Portland. Though she had to share, that space was huge, nearly three times the size of this cottage.

She intended to stay the entire three months, since the agency made it clear there would be no refund.

With her coffee mug, she walked out amongst the early morning crowd. She'd noticed already that the people gathering for sunrise were considerably different from the sunset crowd. Kiley loved both times but was probably partial to sunsets. Nothing in Portland, even before or after a big rainstorm, looked even vaguely similar.

She began scanning for interesting shells and soon came upon the place where she'd sat last night, recognizing the divots her feet had made in the now-warm sand. As if retracing her steps while investigating for clues, she sat in the exact same location, even placing her feet into the craters of sand.

There were several pelicans soaring over the calm waters this morning. After becoming more interested in a particular area, they would fly up twenty or thirty feet and then dive into the water, smashing their foreheads against the water's surface. Her mother told her they had extra bone in their skulls for this very reason. The awkward snow-white bird floated along the surface for a few seconds, securing and probably eating part of the fish he'd caught. Then he took off toward land, bringing breakfast to his young and his mate.

She studied the beach people, devoid of children at the present time. Groups of colorful joggers drifted past her as she sat and enjoyed the morning. Sipping her coffee, she prepared to go inside and work on her deadline, her spirits brightened. Kiley could almost envision a day when she could finally relax and enjoy the beach community of her childhood.

She thought about the plaque she'd brought with her.

The beach heals everything. The message hit her right in the middle of her chest. She could feel the sheer terror this poor young woman was going through. If she was still alive, and that was a big if, she'd be locked up, confined to a cage somewhere. She'd be defenseless, probably naked, the end of her suffering beginning to be the one thing she'd most desire. The girl was a long way from the home of her childhood and probably convinced no one was even interested in looking for her.

Kiley allowed only a sliver of that fear to slip in, and then she shut off those thoughts. Given the choice of living in a cage or being killed, she wasn't sure which option she could face.

Maybe I should just stay here forever.

CHAPTER 5

"**H**EY, JASON, KYLE told me you were out here. How's it hangin'?" barked the voice of Andy Carr, one of his Brothers from SEAL Team 3 in Coronado.

"I'm good. I'm good. That's right. You're detached now. Are you here?"

"Almost detached. Waiting for the paperwork. Hell yes, I'm here."

"You bought a little place here," Jason said into his cell. "How close are you to Sunset Beach?"

"Fuck you, Jason. That's where I'm living, man."

"I apologize then. I could have had you join me when I freed Thomas."

Andy cleared his throat. "I was partly calling about that. So you did the deed, then?"

"Last night, at dusk."

Neither man said anything for a few minutes. Jason watched a young, sunburned red-headed boy of about ten skim the flat surf on a boogie board strapped to his ankle.

"I'm sorry I missed it. But I'm glad you gave him a proper sendoff. Thanks for doing that."

"Yup. It's what we do." He was surprised to experience a tear slipping down his cheek. He flicked it away with his thumb and forefinger.

"So where at Sunset are you staying? If I'd have had half a brain, I would have insisted you stay with us."

"I'm slightly south. St. Pete's."

"Ah, man. You're paying nosebleed rates. How long are you staying?"

"I was thinking about five, six days."

"Well, that settles it. Bring all your gear and come on over. Don't argue, 'cause Aimee will kick your butt. Just check out and come on. You're like five, ten minutes away at high traffic."

"I don't want to impose."

"God, Jason. I feel totally like a stoned teenager to have missed what you were doing. I probably even saw you walking down the beach, and it just never registered, man."

"No worries. I knew you had a place nearby. It was cool the way it worked out. It was just him and me. Like it always was." Jason decided to leave out his conversations with Thomas from inside the urn or the words of his ancestors. Andy would never understand things like this.

"You lie well, Jason. Now get your stuff, and Aimee and I will give you the grand tour. You probably got sick of hearing me talk about it."

Jason chuckled.

"It's right on the beach. Probably not as nice as Hawaii, but she and I make a pretty good team, and we're thinking of making the arrangement permanent."

"Thought you were going up to Little Creek."

"I am. Team 4 is deployed right now, so I have a little time before we re-hook up."

"Where is their theater?"

"Oh, it's all over the place. They've been doing some stuff in South America and the Caribbean. Mexico. I'm hoping it will be a good fit. They lost their senior medic a year ago evacuating some embassy staff and friendlies in Venezuela. Everyone on that squad is new, so Kyle wants me to push it and grab that job. He's tight with their LPO, Peterson."

"Good. Well, it sounds like you've got a plan. I liked Aimee that one time I met her at the party."

"Quit talking and get over here, Jason. I'll start fixing lunch."

The clerk at the front desk grilled him about his desire to check out early. "Did you find another place discounting their rooms? There's a lot of that going on.

I have authorization to match any deal they offered you."

"No, sir. I ran into a buddy, and he won't take no for an answer. I knew he was in the area, but he called me just now, and he's insisting. Sorry, man."

"Well, that I can't match. But I will do this for you. I won't charge you an early cancellation fee if you promise to give us a try next time you're out here. How's that?"

"More than fair. Done deal."

Jason held the slip of paper he'd written the address on in his right hand, steering the Hummer with his left. In less than five minutes, he was slowly driving down a narrow alleyway over white sand and crushed shells. He saw Andy standing outside a garage door with a couple of beers in his hands.

The house had recently been painted a coral-red color with off-white trim. New windows had been installed on the second and third floors. A concrete mixer and some tools were propped against the other garage door. Bags of concrete were stacked several high.

Andy insisted on handing Jason a beer first, and then they hugged. He peered into the truck. "Where's your stuff?"

"Just a duffel in the back. No firepower."

"Really?"

"Oh, I'm packin', just didn't bring any of my long guns." Jason was quick to correct Andy's misconception. He didn't know anyone who didn't travel armed. Most of the SEAL wives and girlfriends did as well. Where it was illegal to carry, they were more careful. But it didn't change their behavior one bit.

Jason hooked the duffel over his shoulder and presented Andy with a bottle of wine he'd bought at the bar at the hotel.

"I know jack about wine, but they told me it was good," Jason said.

Andy tucked it under his arm and showed the way to a new glass front door. Once inside, the faint smell of paint and other odors stubbornly clung to the air.

"So, we knocked out the ceiling here and made this catwalk with landings going up to the second and third floor rooms."

Jason admired the woodwork. Bleached and tumbled by the ocean, lightly sanded and varnished with a clear coat, the finish taking on the color of driftwood. He smoothed his fingers over the handrail and spindles made from pieces of wood in varying sizes.

"I like the way this feels. This almost looks like driftwood," he said.

"Well, it kinda is. Everything in here is recycled, except for the windows and the roof and some of the hardware. Even some of that came from a salvage yard.

They find all sorts of shit after those hurricanes. People go along and collect all this stuff, throw away the garbage, and clean up and re-sell some of the metal, tile, and wood. Lots of wood."

The pattern on the handrails was totally random, some pieces laying at an angle, some vertical, and others horizontal, which reminded Jason of the old Hawaiian plantation designs he'd seen at museums growing up. Interspersed here and there were rusted pieces from the insides of machinery. They'd used gears, car parts, pieces from the backs of wooden chairs, and metal railings, all making an eclectic patchwork design. One panel even held an old rusty hand saw. On the second floor was a cozy platform with an overstuffed couch placed to take advantage of the ocean view. There appeared to be two bedrooms on that floor, and following the stairs up to the third floor, Jason guessed it was a master suite that covered the entire space.

One side of the living room had a recycled glass and metal garage door opening to the beach and ocean beyond. With chains on either side, the door would roll up and could be secured there, exposing the living room directly to the outside.

"Where did you guys find this place?" Jason asked.

"Actually, Aimee found it. I'll let her tell you the story. We just put a little down, and did a lease option.

We're using the cash to do the work, and then we'll get a loan to cash the former owner out."

"So I guess you're staying, then." Jason noted that he'd never seen Andy so happy.

"Fuckin' A. Nothing could tear me away from this place. I'll fly up to Little Creek, but I'll be back here every chance I can. I'll be one of those *one and dones.*

"You impress me, brother." Jason said, taking a long drag on his beer. "Going all domestic and only after one deployment."

"I have over three years left. But, when you meet the right woman, it changes you. So it's not my fault!" Andy was grinning, wiggling his eyebrows up and down. "You remember Cory Phillips?"

"Yeah I've met him a couple of times." Word had spread quickly about all of Cory's problems, and Jason thought he'd been booted out.

"Cory grew up here. I think he knew Thomas."

"No kidding? Where is Cory now? He's on Team 8, right?" He was trying to be polite and show some respect.

"Four. He was four. I'll be joining up with his old team. Kyle helped set it up and said they were a good group. Anyway, Cory's coming here for a couple of days. You'll get to see him. He's been in San Antonio at the burn center."

"Oh, I'm so sorry. I didn't hear about that. How

bad is it?" Cory's battle with drugs, alcohol, and gambling, as well as other vices were legendary, but he didn't want to add credence to the rumors. Jason hoped his injuries weren't major.

"Not a patient. He's taking the burn course rotation. It's a one-year billet like the long medic course. Then he'll probably re-engage with Team 4. It came at the right time. Cory pulled things out at the last minute. He sounds great on the phone."

Andy looked up and spotted Aimee coming through the front door.

"Who sounds great?" she asked. She gave him a big smile.

She was carrying groceries, so Jason scurried toward her, took the two brown bags from her arms and set them on the kitchen counter. Aimee thanked him and approached Andy.

"Who were you talking about, sweetheart?" she asked again.

"Cory. He's stopping by later. He just called." Andy embraced her. "And look who else I dug up!"

"I see," she said. "Looks like my plans to finish painting the guest room are flying out the window."

Jason began to chuckle. "Good job, Andy. Invite me over to keep from having to get your hands dirty."

"Not true. I cry foul!" Andy protested.

Aimee tilted her forehead in Jason's direction.

"We're delighted you stopped by. This sort of thing happens every day, so no worries. I'm more than used to it."

"You've done a beautiful job, Aimee. It's going to be magnificent."

Jason could see she appreciated hearing that. She studied the beams above her head and the filtering light coming from clearstory windows placed around the perimeter of the upper ridge. The area reminded him of a crow's nest.

"Some days, it almost feels like a church," she answered. "So you're still at Coronado, right?" Her lavender eyes sparkled in the late morning sun.

"Yes, ma'am."

"Jason came out to do Thomas' honor flight. They were very close," Andy added.

"Oh yes. That was awful. All the locals remember him. They've plastered pictures of him over several of the hangouts." She examined her feet, and then flashed those lavender eyes at him again. "I'm so glad you could be there for him."

The conversation came to an awkward close. Jason quickly added, "He'd have done the same for me. He didn't have family."

"We were his family," added Andy.

"Indeed." Jason held his beer up, toasting it in the air, an action Andy mirrored, just before they finished off their bottles.

CORY ARRIVED JUST after they'd finished lunch. Jason hadn't remembered him being such a clown. He teased and danced around Aimee, making her laugh. On several occasions she blushed. He was respectful, but Jason could tell Cory had stopped by to see Aimee, more than Andy.

His former team buddy pulled him aside.

"I should explain that Cory and Aimee have some history." Jason could see pain in Andy's eyes. "In fact, they were together when I met her."

Jason shoved his eyebrows nearly to his hairline. "Whoa. That's a bit awkward."

"It's cool. But I'm just explaining why I give him some liberties. He's done a good job so far. If he crosses the line, I'll put him in his place. But Aimee will always be a friend, and I wouldn't want it any other way."

"You're a better man than me, Andy."

"Nah, I just love her. That's all."

"So when's the wedding?"

"Listen to you! We've been so busy getting this place ready. But I wouldn't have put in for the transfer if we hadn't talked about it and agreed. Probably next year."

Jason knew why Andy didn't have a date. Aimee hadn't fully decided to marry him yet. But he was going to hold back on telling Andy and let him figure it out for himself.

"You're a smart man, Andy. The woman always decides," he said.

Andy sighed, watching the two friends laughing in the kitchen while Aimee was cleaning up. "Ain't that the truth?" Then he asked, "What about you? Anyone you've got tucked away somewhere?"

"You know me. I'm a little slow when it comes to all that. But I have my eye out for something special."

"As in here, in Florida or California?"

"None of your fuckin' business, asshole," Jason whispered.

They both laughed.

"You know, Damon's out here. He and Martel are coming over Wednesday night for a little party. It will be a nice little reunion. If you dare bring that *Something Special* around, I'd like to meet her."

"We'll see. Way too premature at this point. But I'll work on it."

"You do that. You work on that hard." He gave Jason a crazy grin. I'm counting on you. One by one we're all dropping like flies. I think you're next."

"Don't count your chickens. But, if I don't come back tonight, don't wait up for me, okay, sweetie?"

Andy punched him in the arm.

"Oh, so she lives at the beach."

"I don't know where she lives, but I'm going to find out."

Jason didn't want to answer any more questions, so he asked if Andy wanted to join him for a walk on the beach. He needed to get away from what was beginning to feel slightly restrictive.

"Go for it. I'm going to stay behind this time. It's going to get beautiful out there in about an hour."

"Yesterday was breathtaking." Jason could still see the bright orange glow in the back of his mind. He was anxious to replay, if not relive some of that encounter.

Aimee broke away from the kitchen to lead him upstairs, giving him one of the two rooms on the Gulf side. "Cory will either sleep on the couch downstairs or up here in the other guest room. But I'm warning you. He snores, although maybe now not so much. He's stopped drinking."

"So I've heard. Good for him. That's not an easy thing to do. You and Andy must have helped with that."

"Timing. Everything is timing," she said before she left the room.

Jason hung up a shirt he'd brought, laid out his shaving gear, then put on a light-weight windbreaker, and headed to the surf.

He thought about Aimee's comment.

Everything is timing, isn't it, Thomas?

Instantly, he was transported to Africa, the Nigerian village that caused all the carnage. The mission suddenly became doomed in failure when an elder objected to the SEALs evacuating young girls who had essentially been brought to the village as slaves and were to be married off to some of the older, more wealthy members. The "brides" were a gift from a local warlord, in exchange for their cooperation.

State didn't have all their facts in order. He'd been told it wouldn't be the last time they'd sacrifice their lives for faulty intel. But, at best, what had been a very tricky op, now ratcheted up ten clicks, with no one to help the little squad who had been sent out to pick up the girls. They'd learned, in a life or death situation not to rely on the local Afrika Corps. And since it was thought that too much of a show of force would draw out the bad guys, they had a skeleton crew. That meant shooters and medics.

But in fact, the opposite turned out to be true that day. In the shootout that occurred, two girls were re-captured, two others were killed, half of Kwanda Freescott's men were incapacitated, while the leader and the two girls retreated back into the brush and disappeared.

Afterwards, Thomas was helping one of the girls into the back of the van they were using when a sniper picked him off with a glancing shot to the head that did enough damage to end his life. Jason was there within seconds, regardless of his own safety. He held Thomas, told him the evac team was on its way, described the land where he was going and how there would be greeters to welcome him, and urged him not to be afraid.

As his best friend's life drifted away, Jason wept. Even in the community of brothers so tightly woven together into the tapestry of that force for good, he felt all alone for the first time.

HE'D BEEN SITTING just past the surf, watching the oranges swirl and outline the billowy clouds. Jason could see how Thomas would love it here. It wouldn't bring his friend back, but he decided to explore the community, just as if his friend was doing it himself. He owed that to him. The two of them had talked about spending some time on Kauai, but Jason never got the chance to share his ancestral home.

Another lifetime, brother.

He sensed someone was behind him and turned, finding the woman he was hoping to see at the beach tonight.

He scrambled to stand, but she stopped him.

"No! Don't get up," she said. Her nerves were still on edge. But, without the floppy hat and the huge sunglasses, the woman he saw in front of him was a vibrant, natural beauty. His body immediately warmed to her presence, as it had done last night.

"Then come, join me," he said in a whisper.

She halted and, thinking better of it, slowly took a seat where he'd been sitting. He gave her space right next to him.

"I'm Kiley," she said as she extended her hand.

He placed one palm beneath hers and then the other on top. "I'm Jason." After giving her a slight squeeze, he withdrew, placing his hands in his lap. He was going to move very slowly, since he didn't want to raise her fears again.

"I came down here when I saw you, because I still feel I need to apologize for my behavior last night."

"Don't worry. You don't owe me anything. I probably came on too strong, but I wanted to convince you that I had no ill intentions."

She nodded. "No, I was the idiot." She let out a huge sigh. "My life has been a basket of snakes, lately."

Jason hated snakes.

"You don't have to tell me anything, Kiley. I just want you to be safe. I don't really need all the details."

"Of course you don't. Why would you?"

Her comment was a bit on the snarky side and Jason didn't like the tone. He squinted, looking down on her, wrinkling his brow. She was damned hard to figure out. He decided he better stop trying. He sensed something might be wrong with her or her situation. She was damaged, somehow.

"I'm sorry. I can't seem to help lashing out at you. It isn't you; it's my situation. But that's all I'm going to say."

He didn't believe her. "You sure?" He grinned at her shocked expression. "For someone who doesn't want to talk about it, you seem to bring it up a lot."

She attempted to get to her feet. He'd just pushed her over the edge.

Dammit!

He held onto her forearm, but only with enough firmness to let her know he wasn't going to let go. If she insisted, of course he would do so. He wanted to make it clear she still had the control.

"Stay. Don't go."

It was too awkward for her to continue to rise, so she collapsed back down onto the sand, and withdrew her arm from his grip.

"Can we start all over?" he asked.

Looking into her warm eyes, he saw intelligence, honor, strength and something else he couldn't quite figure out.

She nodded, not looking at him.

"Where would you like to restart this from?" he asked.

Her glance at his lips gave him a most delicious

signal. He slowly moved his face closer to hers until he was about two inches from her. He licked his lips and then pressed them against hers. He felt her jolt, and then soften to him.

He separated and angled his chin in the opposite direction. She matched his movement and met him halfway again, where their lips touched. She opened to him but he didn't take advantage.

Instead, he cupped her cheek with his hand, stroking down the side of her face, his fingers sifting through her hair.

Should I stop?

He was fairly certain she'd agree to anything he asked of her. The idea thrilled him. And he understood what a gift that was.

She held his hand in both of hers and kissed his palm. "Come inside. With me," she whispered. "Please?"

Her shyness moved him. He was falling off a cliff like one of those deep dives off the rocks back home. His body was soaring through the sky as if he was a bird.

They held hands as she led them to a bungalow three houses to the left of the beach access path. She pressed her back against her sliding glass window, and before letting him inside, she drew her arms up around his neck and pulled him down to her in a full-blown passionate kiss that lasted several minutes. His hands roamed down her backside, and over her arms, while his kisses were placed under her chin and beneath her ear. He loved her faint flowery scent and the way her delicate breathing grew strong and robust, as the woman came alive in his arms.

He pressed her lower torso to his hardened groin, and she moaned into his ear.

She broke off their embrace, opened the door, and stepped backward into her living room. He followed her every movement and closed the door behind him.

The interior of the little home smelled like her. She had a candle burning on the kitchen counter, which gave off a golden angel-light. But his eyes were focused on the movement of her body as she continued to walk backwards, drawing him into the bedroom, where she dropped his hand and began to remove her top.

He stopped her.

"Let me," he whispered, kissing her ear. "I want to do it all."

"Oh my God," she sighed before she wrapped her arms around his neck and shoulder and drew her knees up around his waist.

He chuckled. "Clothes are awkward. If you'll just have a little patience, I'll have you naked and wet in two minutes. And that's being slow."

His fingers probed the waistband of her jeans, sliding over her smooth buttocks. Once, again, he drew her in, and showed her what a good fit they were, and once again, she moaned.

He pulled her oversized tee shirt over her head, as she undid his fly. Her fingers found him just as he removed her bra. She slipped his pants down over his hips just before he knelt in front of her, slowly sliding her jeans over her well-developed hips. The scent of her arousal caused a deep pounding in his chest. He placed one hand between her legs, and lazily let his forefinger travel the length of her opening, spreading her moisture.

With her hands pressed into the tops of his shoulders she leaned forward and widened her knees, allowing him access to slowly insert two fingers. He kissed her breasts and then let his tongue leave a trail down to her belly button as her breathing became ragged. She gripped his shoulders nearly to the point of causing him pain.

On his haunches, he leaned back to observe her arousal as his fingers slid in and around her opening. Her eyes were shut, her lips flushed out into a plump O, driving the need to taste her. She widened her stance farther, mewling soft squeals as his tongue probed and drank from her elixir. His tiny lapping movements made her shudder. She squeezed her right breast, keeping her grip tightly onto his left shoulder. She seemed starved for what he fully intended on giving her.

Abruptly, he picked her naked body up, and walked her on his knees onto the bed. His fingers splayed out and touched her perfect body. His knee nudged between her legs and she raised one thigh, arching to meet him. He crawled up over her, placing his hand under her neck and then holding her head while he devoured those lips, giving back the same intensity he was dishing out.

He angled his hips, his growing erection persistently working against the lips of her sex, probing and testing for an opening. When at last he found her, he moved his arm to the arch in her lower back, elevating her pelvis so he could thrust deep, holding her tight against him.

Jason had not thought to ask her about protection, so he stopped. Her body began to move beneath him, her hands gripping his butt cheeks, begging him to go deeper. He leaned over and whispered, "Should I—?"

But she put her hand over his mouth. She stared into his eyes.

"Fuck me."

"Yes ma'am."

CHAPTER 6

WAKING UP IN the pink glow of early morning, with his huge, muscled, and fully sleeved arm still holding her body against his hip was awkward. The level of feasting on each other's passions was so intense she wasn't sure she could look him in the eyes. He had demanded she show him how to please her. He guided her to what he wanted her to do. Though her pheromones were raging wildly, it was the most intentional lovemaking she'd ever had. His body was a lovemaking machine.

She felt his tongue touch the side of her neck before she felt his enormous hands capture and claim her left breast. He squeezed her nipple, which made her arch up and feel the dull ache for him again, spiking her body back to life.

Because he was so massively strong, he had no trouble moving her body up and over him, planting her on his cock, maneuvering her up and down just the way he needed it. With her eyes closed, she focused on the feel of his girth, on the sweat forming inside her thighs as they moved together.

"Open your eyes, Kiley," he whispered, still moving her slowly up and down on him.

She timidly obeyed. She'd never found it so hard to make eye contact with a sexual partner. Jason demanded it.

As if he knew what she was thinking, he murmured, "I like to watch it on your face when you come."

The wave of pleasure flooded over her like the ocean, tickling and sparking every cell in her body. She moved her knees, bringing her legs in front, sinking in deeper to his thrusting motion beneath her.

Her eyes began to flutter as if she was going to faint, but it was her body's warning. She was about to experience an orgasm unlike she'd ever felt before.

Jason sat up, bringing her with him, and then pressed her back into the bed. Moving her legs to his shoulders, he undulated his hips in a circular back and forth that coated and touched everywhere inside her channel.

She threw her head from side to side, and then rose her chin to the ceiling as he picked up the pace. He stopped long enough to caress her neck with his probing fingers, following up with soft kisses. He gently bit her earlobe. She grabbed his ass with her right hand and squeezed as hard as she could. He drilled her deep, relentlessly, and at last slowed so she could feel her own orgasm punching into motion, milking him. Her moans spurred him on, pressing her limits and making her explode. Her body shuddered with full release.

In between thrusts his sweet kisses continued the slow burn as her body completely gave him all the power.

Finally, his heart-breaking moan claimed whatever holdback she had felt, when he released into her. His fingers clutched at her scalp as if needing to attach. His other hand rose her pelvis up to receive every drop he had to give.

The healing, sensuous dance didn't satisfy her. She was hungry for more. It was the perfect way to begin a day.

After their breathing slowed, he carefully extricated himself from the tangle of sheets and her limbs, returning with a cool towel. The damp cloth felt heavenly as he began to dab her forehead. She felt delirious with the levels of abandon he'd brought her to. His warm smile as he worked to soothe her burn was something she couldn't take her eyes off of. He gently spread her legs and held the cool towel against her swollen lips, and then gently kissed her.

Who was this man? Where on the planet had he come from? The right side of his body was completely covered in tats, designs with parallel lines and swirls she was certain meant something. Everything about him was sculpted and toned as if he was a bodybuilder. His thighs were larger than the diameter of her waist. When he walked, she could see muscles in his butt cheeks flex and release. She held the towel between her legs, mesmerized by the sight of him.

"You okay, Kiley? I didn't hurt you, did I?"

"No." It was all she could say.

"You want some help with that?" he nodded to the towel he'd given over to her.

She didn't know how to answer. She finally burst out laughing. "You've taken all my words away, Jason." It really was funny, this effect he'd had on her. "I'm a newspaper reporter and I don't have a thing to say."

He lay on his side next to her, propping his head up with his elbow, and lazily ran his fingers up and down her midsection. There were no sexual parts there, but the movement itself was so stimulating, she had the urge to kiss him again.

She touched his cheek. Her forehead leaned against his. Their legs were still entangled.

"Tell me something," he whispered.

She pressed her forefinger over his mouth, rubbing back and forth.

"Tell you what?" she whispered as she watched her finger travel over the fullness of those lips that could drive her wild.

"Tell me how you feel."

She palmed his cheek, drew her face to his, and whispered. "Like you've charmed me with a spell I will not recover from."

His fingers stopped sifting through her hair, and for a few seconds, she thought perhaps she'd said something wrong. Then his face broke out into a wicked grin.

"What?" she softly demanded. She studied the designs that covered his shoulder and upper arms, the pads of her fingers traveling over the exquisite artwork as if it was a relief.

"I'm a medic. So I will bring you to the edge and then a little further. And then I'll catch you when you fall. I'll work my magic on you, revive you, and make you need my healing ways."

She blinked. It was a strange answer. But it completely fit.

"So you are addicted then? Is that what you're saying?" She continued touching his lips.

"I hope so. As I think you are to me, Kiley. I like the way you taste, the way you move. I like what you show me in your eyes and in your heart."

She nodded, even though she was incapable of any

serious concentration. "What are all these designs?"

"They're warrior designs. Some of these patterns have covered the men of my family for generations."

"Are you a warrior, Jason?"

"I am."

"For real?"

"I am."

"Like a cage fighter or something?"

He rolled over on his back, laughing so hard he began to cry. With his arm over his forehead, she noted that they were the size of her thighs. The lines almost appeared to come alive as the muscles moved underneath. Even his belly laugh was sexy.

"You obviously work out," she posed.

"Yes, I do. I do every day."

"Like you pull trucks by rope with your bare hands or something? You do—what?—a hundred sit-ups without getting winded? Could you pick up this bed and hold it over your head?"

"I've never tried those things." He rose up just enough to kiss her again. "I get to do cool stuff. I'm a man of action. That's what we call it."

"We? You part of some alien space force or something?"

"Hardly, Kiley. I'm just a man."

"Just a man you say. *Just* a man. You made love like five times last night. Now I suppose you'll tell me the bad news. You're part of some ancient brotherhood cult and you run naked and throw telephone poles."

"Now, that I've actually done. Well, with some help from my friends."

"Do your friends look like you?"

"No. We're all different. We come from all over the world."

"You all have these markings?" she asked.

"Well, some of us do. Not like these, though. And I don't run naked down the beach, but some probably have. But these types of tats are special. These are a chronicle of my heritage, my Polynesian ancestral heritage, Kiley. So, someone else's would be different."

"So, what are you, a big soccer team?" She knew that was wrong. "Maybe not soccer. Soccer players are skinny. But how about Rugby then?"

"I love Rugby. We have a Hawaiian form of Rugby that's even more challenging. And there's a famous Rugby team who do Maori chanting before their games. Ever heard of the All Blacks Haka?"

"The what?"

"It's a Maori All Blacks Haka. I've watched them several times. They do this chant that scares the liver out of the opposition."

Kiley had never known a Rugby player.

"So are you a sports figure of some kind?"

"No."

He knew she was pressing for answers and wasn't going to give her any until he was good and ready to. She hoped that he wasn't going to keep secrets, but she'd play along for a bit.

"I know," she giggled. "You're a personal trainer!"

His eyes roamed down her frontside. He angled his head to take a different view. "Would you like that?"

"I think I'd find it distracting," she said, avoiding his eyes. "I'd probably drop the weights on my foot, something like that."

"Why do you say that?" He gently brushed the hair from her face.

"I'm just a klutz, that's all. Not very coordinated."

"It's just a matter of training. With focus and discipline, you can make your body do anything you want it to do."

"Can you heal the dead?"

She realized right away the mistake she'd made. He sat up and turned his back to her.

"Jason, I'm sorry about that comment. That was stupid of me. I wasn't thinking."

"It's okay," he said to his lap.

But she could tell something was eating a hole in his heart. She waited. Finally, he turned, flipping onto his stomach and peered into her eyes.

"I'd give anything to be able to do that. Life is random. We do the best we can, but sometimes, that's not good enough. He didn't have to die. He shouldn't have died. But he did, and I was spared. There have been times when I've beat myself up about that. But it is what it is."

"And you're going to honor him by living well," she said, stroking his forearm. She let her fingers mate with his, examining the roughness, the cuts and divots made in his flesh. He used his hands for something, and he obviously worked hard. She drew his palm to her cheek and held it there, returning his gaze.

Then she drew his hand down her frontside, guiding him to the juncture between her legs. She felt shy all of a sudden.

"Sorry."

"You sure apologize a lot, Kiley. Don't ever apologize for things you don't mean to. It's the way you are. And…" he said as he placed his hand under her thigh and bent her knee, "I find you perfect just the way you are. This is magic," he said before he kissed her belly button. "And I'm in the mood for a whole lot more."

KILEY'S CELL PHONE rang, waking them up. It was Carmen. She took the call in the living room.

"Hey there," she whispered. "So Newman put you on the story."

"Was that your doing? Because I'm not happy." Carmen was smart, but Kiley had always felt their communications started way too adversarial. "He should have finished your work instead of taking me off my desk."

"Between you and me, Carmen, he'd have fucked it up, and you know this."

"I don't dig seeing naked women horribly brutalized and left for dead, Kiley. I cannot understand how you get off on that shit."

She could tell changing her mind was going to be a waste of time, so she didn't argue with her. "Just give it a few days, and if you can't, you can't." She sighed. "And for the record, I don't get off on it. I'm trying to see to it that it stops happening."

"Well, there you go again. Saving the world, Kiley. That's not my gig. I don't want to dig into the crap, seedy underbelly of society. I want to experience the excitement of life, not muck around in detritus. Look, it's not that I can't. I don't want to."

"But you've always been in favor of defending the little guy. That's what you're all about, Carmen. This is a wrong that has to be exposed."

"Yeah, is that what you're doing? Run off to lie on the beach in Florida?"

Panic began to seep into her veins with a cold fear that someone, probably her editor, had not kept her secret safe. The betrayal hurt.

"Who told you that?"

"Everyone knows, Kiley."

"In just a couple of days, I'll be sending in the end of the series. Then I'm going to turn in all my notes to the police and let them do the rest. After that, I'll be coming back. You just do your investigation and feed me some of the facts, and I'll help steer you where I think your investigation has promise. I've spent a lot of time studying this whole ring of bad boys. I've even met many of the players."

"Is it true someone killed your cat?" Carmen asked.

"Yes. And slashed my tire."

"And you don't think I'd be in any danger, Kiley?"

"Not after I publish my story. But you'll have all the background to do a killer follow-up. That's something I'm just handing you, Carmen. If we expose this ring and get the light of justice shining down on them, you'd be helping the community. Heck, you might even get a medal for it. There could be a Pulitzer in it for you."

Carmen agreed to scan and send pictures and a copy of the reports on file. Kiley gave her a couple of women's shelters she could go interview, including the name of one of her sources who had been nearly killed in a botched trafficking event.

"I'll call you back in two days, and if you have questions, put them in an email. No messaging. I won't have this phone when I call back, so don't try, okay?"

"Geez, this is all very cloak and dagger-like."

A dark cloud of worry fell over Kiley when she considered that perhaps Carmen hadn't taken her cautions seriously enough.

"Be smart. Don't talk about it to anybody but Corbin, and even then, don't tell him everything. Don't leave your notes around your apartment or at your desk at the paper. If we're careful, we could be doing a really great thing for the Portland community. But it also extends way beyond our city."

"I'm on it. Look for that email in an hour or so, Kiley."

"Thanks. You're going to be great. Oh, and Carmen, no more talk about Florida. I'm not there. That was just a ruse."

"Okay, if you say so." Carmen hung up.

When Kiley turned around, Jason was standing against the wall, his arms crossed over his chest. He didn't look happy.

She wondered how much of her conversation Jason heard. Before she could try to give an explanation, he straightened up, his fists clenched at his sides.

"What the hell are you into, Kiley?"

"I can explain, Jason. I can explain it all—well, most of it, anyway."

"You fuckin' better. Just answer this question first, are you doing anything illegal here, because if you are,

I cannot be involved. And I can't know anything about it."

"No. Come. Sit down, and I'll tell you what I can."

He sat across the coffee table from her, again crossing his chest with his arms, waiting.

"I'm working on a story for the *Columbia Passage*. That's the big newspaper in Portland, where I live. I've uncovered some facts about a human smuggling ring operating out of several shelters in the area. I've been working on this story now for nearly two years. And I've so far published three installments. I'm about to publish the last one, but before I could get it done, I started getting death threats by phone. I got some letters at the office too. Someone broke into my apartment and trashed the place. Luckily, neither I nor my roommate were home at the time."

"Who did this?"

"The police said kids."

"And why don't you believe them?"

"Because, Jason, they cut up my cat. They gutted him and left him on the couch. It was horrible. And then the next day, someone slashed one of my tires at the paper.

"But you don't know specifically who."

"We have problems with street gangs in Portland like every big city in the U.S. I think some of the City staff are somehow connected. There are some city-sponsored women's shelters created by the Mayor and his task force. But they may not be so innocent as far as how they handle teen runaways and battered women. They have a lot of young immigrant girls. And my research has led me to believe there are organized crime figures involved. They might have compromised certain city officials, too. My editor says the Mayor has asked that I stop publishing the stories, that it sheds a negative light on their good works. He also said it might be dangerous—to me."

"He actually said that?"

"He told my editor he got an anonymous call. It was a warning."

"That's an understatement. You have police involved, right?"

"Only for the burglary. They filed it primarily as an animal cruelty case since nothing was taken. That's all. I didn't offer anything about the investigation I was doing. I guess they didn't put it together, so not really. Not yet at least."

"Kiley, this is absurd. You can't take this on all by yourself."

"I've got the backing of the paper on this. The power of the press and public opinion will definitely be on my side after I'm finished. I just want to lay out the evidence so the public sees everything. If I go to the officials, they'll find some way to bury it. I know they will. But if I get the public on their cases, we have a much better shot at exposing them and hopefully getting them rooted out."

"This is your plan?"

"Well yes, that's my plan."

"Fuck."

"Hey, that's not nice."

"Somebody's gotta tell you the truth. How the heck did you get involved in this story?"

She sucked in air, proud that she'd been trusted with this very important assignment. "My editor gave it to me for a series on runaway girls in the Portland area, except that the more I looked into things, the wider my search became. The story started out about a young illegal immigrant disappearing. But now we're looking at ten missing girls. Only four of them have been found. I've got to wrap this up, finish my story, and then lie low for a while."

"You think? Like forever."

"I hope not."

"So that's what you do. You're an investigative journalist?"

"Yes."

"And you thought, when I met you at the beach, what? I was one of the bad guys, like a hit man?"

She avoided his stare.

"Look at me, Kiley. Is that what you thought? I

mean you were *that* scared?"

"Well, yes. Jason, I'm probably blowing it out of proportion. But my mind just isn't letting me relax, so I've been seeing bad guys everywhere. I finally had to leave Portland and go somewhere I felt safe."

He shook his head.

"Unbelievable," he mumbled. "You're wrong, Kiley. There are no safe places. I've seen firsthand what these cabals do. I've seen what lengths they'll go to keep anyone from interrupting their operation. You do not want to be messing with them. Trust me on that."

Kiley sat back. A whole new set of questions started flashing in her mind.

She began slowly, needing to unpack her concerns, one question at a time. It was rather backwards, she realized. Here she'd slept with the man, and now she wanted to know who he was. Her *Aunt Itoldyouso* was having a temper tantrum inside her brain.

Kiley, what have you done?

"I know you're not a Rugby player. What exactly is it you do, then?"

"I'm a Navy SEAL."

CHAPTER 7

B Y EARLY AFTERNOON, and they'd basically stayed in bed nearly the whole time, even while she was peppering him with questions about his SEAL training. He was careful to reveal just enough to satisfy her and not lead to more questions. Jason knew he was overdue with the check-in and Andy's house would be wondering where he was. They didn't realize he was a mere six or seven houses down from them.

His concern for Kiley's safety bothered him so much that he needed to make a call to his LPO, Kyle Lansdowne, but out of earshot of Kiley. Although it frustrated Team guys from time to time, they all knew they were prohibited from interfering with any domestic criminal behavior. Recently, the Navy had made examples of SEALs trying to blur that line. He didn't want to be one of the casualties, just because he was trying to help someone do something for the good of society.

Convincing Kiley would be another story, though. She'd already asked for his help, suggesting he be her bodyguard.

"You don't get it. I'm supposed to be working up to our next mission overseas. I can't just take off and play policeman."

She'd agreed with him, but he could see she wasn't happy about it. He needed some guidance. He considered talking to Andy, but since he was on his way to Team 4 and wasn't in a leadership position either, he decided against it. Cory would be a loose cannon. Damon, if he stopped by, would probably be no better.

The other thing that bothered him was that perhaps he'd involved them all too much already. He was certain Kiley had no clue what she was getting into. She had a fantasy about making the world a safer place. That was *his* job, and it involved a hell of a lot more sacrifice than most people would even want to know about. He certainly wasn't going to be the one to tell her. She already had some TV notion of what a SEAL was. And that wasn't her fault. Everyone underestimated and misunderstood them all, but that was how the Teams wanted it to be. The less the general public knew about them the better. If they did their job well, everyone would be safe at home and they'd know nothing about what really lurked outside the borders of the U.S.

He also wasn't suffering under the delusion of complete safety at home, either. He could defend himself and her. He just couldn't go policing society and interfere with his brothers in blue. It was a delicate balance. He had to be careful what he said, and he had to make sure he didn't get involved in anything he could lose his Trident over.

And, as much as he loved their physical relationship, he'd sort of put the cart before the horse. It wasn't wise what he'd done. He had no right staking a claim on her when he didn't really know anything about her.

But over half the guys on the team had violated that one dozens of times. It still was no excuse, though.

She kept looking over at her computer, and he knew she was itching to get back online and file her story.

"Listen, why don't I leave you alone for a few hours?" he asked. "My friends down the beach haven't heard from me since yesterday afternoon. I should check in, and then you can join us down there, or I can return later. How does that sound?"

"You're right. I should get the article written."

"How long do you think you'll be?" he asked.

"Two, three hours. I'll send it off, and then perhaps we can grab some dinner?"

"Sounds like a plan, Kiley."

She began sorting through notes and turned on her

laptop. "Once it's out of my hair, then I will take your suggestion and turn over all my notes and assist the police, if they'll let me."

"Why wouldn't they, Kiley?"

"I don't know. Call it a reporter's instinct. The one thing I've learned about all of this is that things are never what they seem."

"And you don't really know who you can trust."

"Exactly. But my editor thought they'd stop once the stories got published."

Jason knew that was complete folly. But until he had more information on where he stood, profession-ally, he wasn't going to say anything to her.

He wrote down the address of Aimee and Andy's house and handed it to her. "You can't miss it. Think deep pink and red mixed. There isn't anything remote-ly similar in color or intensity."

She took the piece of paper and laid it next to her laptop.

"And you should text me when you head over there so I can watch for you," he added.

She placed her fingers over his mouth. "I will fol-low your instructions to the letter," she said, her arms wrapped around his neck. "Thank you for caring, Jason. I mean that."

"I should be driving you down to the police station, not sitting here listening to your stories. That's the right thing to do, so don't thank me, Kiley."

"It will work out. You'll see. Now that you're here, I'm safe."

Jason bristled at that. "You need anything, anything at all, you let me know. That's my cell." He pointed to the number under the address.

She held his face between her hands. "Didn't you hear me? I'll be fine. You don't have to worry about me."

"I'm going to worry about you plenty. But I like the idea of you being over at the big house. Where I can watch you."

"Thank you. I'll be there before you've had your sixth beer."

Their kiss bordered on some further fooling around, but in the end, they separated. Jason slipped out the sliding glass door and onto the beach.

About halfway to Andy's he dialed Kyle Lansdowne.

"Hey there, Jason. Everything go smoothly?"

"Yessir." He wasn't sure how to begin.

After a minute of air silence, Kyle began, "You know, for a not very talkative guy, you're sure not doing a lot of talking."

Kyle's sixth sense about these things was legendary.

"I met this girl."

"Oh boy. What is it with you guys and Florida? If anything happens to Christy, I'm giving up everything and heading out there. They must put something in the water. And to make matters worse, Christy has been working nearly twenty-four seven. Hell, I'm about to call up Collins and ask him if we could just take a temporary duty to Iraq to go vaccinate some kids or something. At least it would get me out of having kid-duty for the sixth day in a row."

Jason chuckled, "I feel your pain, sir."

"No, you don't. You've got no idea what it's like to be past your prime, hearing about all your guys getting laid and having girl issues. Is that what this call is going to be about? You need more time off so you can cement your relationship? Do you want to know how many times I've gotten that call, son?"

Jason knew he'd calm down, but he just let him rant on. Kyle abruptly laid the phone down to straighten something out. One of his three was crying after he was done.

"Honestly, I don't know how they do this. Tomorrow, I have to take the three of them to a birthday party, one of Maggie's friends. I'm going to strap Brandon to the nearest tree. That means all I'll have to do is watch out for Luke, and at his current age, he still likes girls and thinks they smell nice."

"Well, you give Brandon my best, then. Tell him he should soak in the bathtub, and that will take care of his sore behind."

"Was I that obvious?"

"He's always the one you're talking about getting into trouble, sir."

"Okay. Well, now that we got all that out of the

way, what's the emergency?"

Jason took a deep breath and sat on the bench, donated by the good people of Sunset Beach, about ten steps from the beach access. He watched the constant parade of old and new bodies in various stages of undress and inebriation.

"So this girl is an investigative reporter?"

"Uh-oh. You better run. You didn't say anything you regret, did you?"

"No. Not really."

"Well, which is it—no or not really?"

Jason felt Kyle's mysterious powers of getting anything out of anyone working extremely well.

"The problem is on her end. She's researching a story about the sex trade, and more particularly, she thinks she's identified some key players in a big human smuggling ring up in the Portland area where she lives."

"Okay. I'm holding my breath here."

"She's written some high-profile articles for the Columbian something-or-other."

"Yea. I know it. And?"

"She thinks she's being harassed. Well, she knows she's been harassed. They tossed her place, she's gotten some death threats and the worst part is, they sliced up her cat."

"Holy shit."

"Yeah. Cut up one of her tires too. So, I think she was pretty smart. She hopped on a plane and came to

Florida, where she spent some time as a child."

"Where are her folks? What kind of a father lets his little girl do that stuff?"

"Gone. She's all alone."

"And no ex gunning for her? Jilted or jealous boyfriend?"

"Not that she's mentioned."

"But of course you didn't ask her because you thought it would interfere with your chances of getting laid, right?"

That was a funny line, but Jason held it in. "Actually, we didn't have any problem in that department."

"You've only been there what, two days? God forbid you'd have to wait a week to get in bed with her. So do you want my quick answer or my long answer, Jason?"

"Well, wait. You don't even know the question I'm going to ask you."

"I think I do. I'm a lot smarter than anyone thinks I am. I even let Christy think she's way smarter than me because, well, when a woman feels like she's worshiped, she puts it out like nobody's business."

"Well, you would know, Kyle."

"Watch it. Okay, just humor me. My short answer is run, after you pick your clothes up, that is."

Jason chuckled again. He waited for the long answer.

"My quicker answer is run."

Jason felt cheated. "But…"

"The complicated answer requires a question from me. Is this Miss Have-A-Good-Time or Miss Permanent sort of thing? I mean you guys are all about instalove, so forget that."

"She's in danger, Kyle. And that's what we do. We ride in and save the day."

"In Portland. You're gonna do this in Portland."

"I was thinking if…"

"Are you kidding me? You seriously think that is a good idea?"

"They're gonna kill her, Kyle. I can just sense it."

"And I'm saying I'm going to kill you if you don't stop thinking about it."

Jason had never felt this way. For once, the Navy, his career, his LPO didn't have the answers he wanted them to have.

"Look. What you don't yet know is there's talk of another quick mission, like two weeks max. Back to Benin or Nigeria. And don't go telling the other men. It might happen this week. I can't have you missing your obligation because you're playing private dick in Portland. The timeline's been tentatively moved up. So even if I did give you the green light, you'd have to turn around and fly back here if it was a go. That could happen tomorrow the next day. I'm just staying by the phone. Our ten-day window has shriveled like my grandfather."

"I'd be okay with that."

"And then who would protect her?"

"At that point, I get the police involved."

"Um hum. The same police she doesn't trust now. You think you can pull that off? Seriously, Jason?"

"If it was our only option, and for her safety."

"Personally, I think she better stay there in Florida. I'll grant you a few more days, since you're with the other guys there. Do not breathe a word to anyone."

"I won't. Thanks, Kyle. I have one more question."

"Go ahead." Kyle's voice held exhaustion.

"What if she's working the other end of the same group we've been working with? You remember that guy Colin Riley? He lives in Portland, doesn't he?"

Kyle exhaled. "Because we're not that lucky, Jason."

Saying good-bye, they disconnected. Jason checked his cell, thinking he might have gotten a call while he was talking to Kyle, and discovered it was a text from Andy.

'I'm guessing we're counting chickens, then?'

He texted back. *'I'm right outside your door.'*

'Um. No, you're not. We're on the patio.'

Before him was a familiar circle of friends sitting around a backyard fire pit. Like the parties on the beach at Coronado, they hadn't scrimped on the fire, which sent fingers of flame several feet above the grate.

Damon rose and shook his hand. "Hey, Jason. Thanks for taking good care of old Thomas."

"You bet."

"You remember Martel?"

"I sure do. Didn't come to the wedding, but that

party was hard to forget. Didn't remember too much of it, though."

"No one did," barked Andy.

Jason waved to Aimee and Cory then waited for Martel to take a seat before he sat next to Andy. He addressed Damon first. "Are you hooking up with Team 4 like Andy here?"

"Martel's a teacher. And she's got a dream job neither one of us wants her to give up. But after my billet is done, I'm not re-upping."

Andy sat up straight. "How does that work? You're on one side of the country, and she's on the other?"

"You forget, Andy, I get summers off. It's better to be in San Diego at that time, anyway. Cooler." Martel told him.

"We do rack up the miles some. It's not forever," Damon added.

"Where the hell did you slink off to last night?" Cory barked.

The guy might have his drinking under control, but his mouth was still a problem. Jason wasn't sure he could spend too much time around the man.

Aimee frowned. "Cory, you're being obnoxious."

"Did they work on that elbow in San Antonio?" Andy asked, changing the subject.

"I'm having to get surgery in a couple of months. Doing some PT which is supposed to help. But they're not happy with some of the muscle attachment. Of course, those take longer to heal." Cory looked glum, staring down at his beer.

With one major injury and recovery Cory'd already used up his free bite. He would get rolled, and if he wanted to stay in the Navy, they'd have to give him a desk job. He noticed Andy frowning, probably thinking the same thing.

"How long are you out here?" Damon asked Jason.

"Originally five or six days. But, if I asked for it, I could stay longer."

"Shoot. Rumor has it we might have to go back before the weekend. But Martel's staying, of course. If your friend doesn't work out, I'm sure she can set you up with someone from her school."

It wasn't on Jason's radar. He was distracted by thinking about how Damon knew the trip was going to be cut short.

The rhythm of their banter cascaded all over Jason and it wasn't long before his edginess about being around Cory deflated. He was working on trying to extract Damon's good intel when the ping on his cell phone diverted his attention.

He held his cell up and addressed the crowd. "Looks like she's on her way. You'll get to meet her shortly. I'm going to head down the beach to make sure she doesn't get lost."

Jason jogged barefoot on the warm sand until he saw her small frame coming towards him. When she spotted him, she ran straight into his arms. She hugged him, coming up on tiptoes. Her joyful smile made him happy too.

"You did it, right?" he asked her.

"I did. Waited just long enough to see that my editor got it. Friday, it goes out in the paper and the whole world will know."

"Did you talk to him?"

"No. I'll get the scoop when I call Carmen in a couple of days."

"Good deal."

She turned, pointing. "Look at that sky. You know, I never tire seeing it. I used to miss these colors." Facing him, she continued. "Portland has all those big clouds, the sweeping vistas from the hills surrounding the river, but it rarely has something so absolutely thrilling as that sky."

He wrapped his arms around her, spooning behind. He considered everything Kyle said to him on the phone and brushed it aside.

He decided they'd had enough drama today. It was time for him to show her off to his friends, and then he had plans to create magic all night long. He knew just what he needed to do to chase those fears away.

He heard the chanting again, and that rumble in his belly that told him something spectacular was about to happen.

CHAPTER 8

K ILEY WOKE UP in a panic. She'd been in a dream—
caught in a box-like container at the bottom of the
ocean, the force of the water pressing on her chest. She
began beating against the walls of her confinement and
tried to scream, but no air was coming out. She felt
caught, bound by invisible ties that kept her from
breaking free of the confined space.

She awoke, gasping for air. She was still fighting
until she heard the soft, reassuring voice of Jason
beside her, kissing her, speaking to her in hushed
tones. She still felt like she had to get away. Her heart
felt that he was trying to help her, but her brain would
not loosen the grip of panic. Back and forth she went,
torn between two powerful scenarios, until her fear
took dominance.

She struggled but managed to scramble to her feet,
where she looked down on his shocked expression. Her
arms wrapped around her upper torso as if to protect

her from the man she was sharing a bed with.

He was making his way quickly in her direction, untangling his legs from their sheets, but she warned him.

"Don't! Please, just let me get my bearings." The words didn't even sound like her own. He crouched in front of her. Even that motion made her feel like he was a giant panther, ready to strike without warning.

"Kiley, it was a dream. You're safe."

She couldn't speak.

"It's a panic attack. Brought on by stress, all the things you worry about when you shut down. Happens to all of us in some circumstances. There is no danger here, Kiley."

But she still didn't want him to touch her, to come anywhere near her. She remembered to breathe. He was asking her to breathe, and then she saw him taking in slow, deep breaths and blowing them out, in tandem with her.

As the air refreshed her lungs, new oxygen cleared her brain. Her heartbeat slowed. Looking down on him, she was filled with regret, and began to cry.

His arms were wide. He urged her, "Come to me, Kiley. Let me hold you."

She closed her eyes as black spots began to form in her eyes.

"No!" she shouted at the sickening feeling she was

out of control.

"Just come here, sweetheart."

Tears rolled down her cheeks. Her shoulders slumped, and she collapsed on the bed. Within seconds Jason's warm arms took hold of her as he pulled her up into his chest, rocking her back and forth.

She was mumbling something about having to get out of a box.

"You're safe. I got you, Kiley. There's no box. You're free."

Free!

She lost herself in his warmth, his massive hands rubbing her back to life as he held her and sang to her, his voice lilting. The vibration from his chest seeped into her own until she melted. Melding into his powerful arms, she needed his strength, and felt soothed by his rhythmic whisper-song.

She jerked back to life, her arms seeking him as he continued his chant and the rocking motion forward and back, like she was a tiny ship on a very big ocean. Her fingers touched the smoothness of his skin, pressing into him. Her arms slipped up and around his neck. She floated up into the direction of his voice, her lips desperate to feel the taste of his song.

"Jason!" she gasped.

"Shhh. Shhh. You're safe. Can you hear me, Kiley? You're here right now with me, and you're safe."

"Yes. Love me, Jason. Please make it go away."

"I'm right here, sweetheart."

Their lips collided with need. His fingers worked up the back of her spine, into her hair. His lips caressed her neck, her ear. The more he kissed her the more she felt his fire, his passion.

"You're okay, Kiley. Everything's fine."

"Love me, Jason. Please, love me."

He moaned, holding her so tight she thought perhaps she wouldn't be able to breathe again. Those soft words brought her back to life as his flesh made her body tingle with desire. She was beneath his massive form, her arms at the sides, fingers entangled in fingers, her inner thigh rubbing against his hip, needing him with a burning she'd not felt before.

He inhaled, crouching above her, not pressing into her body, but angling over her. His face down, he leaned closer until he covered her mouth. His tongue sought refuge inside her while his cock pressed, finding the glory trail that led inside her. Inch by slow inch, she felt the power of his pulsing cock, rooting out all doubt and cancelling all her worries.

There was freedom in the way he played her like an instrument, letting her body soar. She grew wings. She drew light from him, her hands touching his patterns and loving the stories there without even knowing what they were. His deep guttural moans sang of welcome satisfaction when he began their descent. He held her shaking body, whispering things she didn't understand until her breathing settled, and she glowed from the feel of his flesh pressing into hers.

He covered them with the bedsheet, still inside her, and commanded her to go back to sleep.

LIGHT FROM THE morning covered her face and chest. She was alone in the bed. She smelled coffee. Opening her eyes, she saw a dark form sitting in the corner of the room, not making a sound. Afraid at first, before she saw him raise a mug to his lips and drink.

She wondered what he was thinking. Was there a dark cloud hanging over his head? Had she ruined her welcome?

"Ready for coffee?" he asked softly.

She sat up, rubbing her eyes and repositioning her hair. "Yes. That would be wonderful."

His naked form, a combination of oversized muscle mass and tiny waist, was just as beautiful to watch from behind as it was to see him come back. His careful hands cupped hers and placed the mug there so it wouldn't tip. He took up a seat next to her. His face stayed close while she drank her first sips. He brushed the hair from her face and studied her, concern creasing his forehead.

"Do you wake up like that a lot?" he asked.

"Just started happening again. I don't remember where I was but it felt so real. No idea what triggered it. I've always been afraid of getting trapped under water or buried alive. It's a dream I used to have when I was a child."

"Can you remember when it started?"

She smiled, remembering playing all afternoon in the lush backyard of her family home. Her mother would let her play there for hours all alone.

"What's the smile for?" he asked.

"I used to have this playhouse, it was an old abandoned greenhouse covered in vines at our old house. We'd moved into a new neighborhood, and I didn't know any of the kids, so my dad repaired it, converting it into my special playhouse and I loved being there." She looked up at Jason. "I felt safe there."

He nodded. "That sounds like a happy memory, not the stuff of nightmares."

"It is." She shook her head. "I mean, it was. It was my sanctuary, and I'd hide there all day. What about you?"

"I used to have a pretend house, a fort, really. I made this special place in the foliage, cutting branches and making room for a private space only I knew how to get into. It had a winding path, completely obscured from the outside so I could sneak in there and watch people walk by, listening to them without being detected. I used to pretend I was on a secret mission."

"Like you do now?"

"No, it's completely different. But I guess the sneaking in and out is the same. I liked knowing I could be very quiet. Learned to hold my breath and avert my eyes so they wouldn't know someone was there. I'd surprise little ground squirrels when they discovered my hiding place."

Kiley took another sip and smiled. She wondered whatever had happened to that little house they left behind when they moved again. Her dad had strengthened it so well it was probably still there, she thought.

"I loved that garden. I had a bedroom that overlooked the yard and the greenhouse. The house had two upstairs bedrooms and two big attics, and while my parents and my brother slept downstairs, I had the whole upper floor to myself. One night, I locked myself in the attic and couldn't get out."

"What did you do?"

"I cried myself to sleep. I spent the night there. I woke up in the morning hearing my mother screaming, thinking I'd been kidnapped. I used to wake up remembering that when I was a kid. Hearing her scream was worse than being alone."

He pressed his palm against her cheek. "I think under stress, perhaps part of that fear gets launched, like some kind of pattern. Don't run away from it. Embrace it until it no longer makes you afraid."

"Jason, I'm so sorry about this morning. I haven't had that dream for years until this week. Not sure why it's coming up now."

"Well, look at the situation you're in. I think it's perfectly understandable, considering." He examined his fingers curled in his lap. "It's a form of stress. We've seen it on the Teams. As medics, we're always on the lookout for someone who doesn't get enough sleep or can't sleep. Perhaps that experience held more trauma than you realized at the time."

"Maybe."

"That's why I want you to consider carefully what you're doing."

"I have."

"I know it's what you're telling yourself what you want to do, but is it really something you can handle, something that is healthy to be involved with?"

She was unclear about his intentions. Did he not understand how important it was for her to do something to save those victims? That she had the power to stop some of it. Surely he didn't expect she could just walk away? Anger began to spread as her heartbeat kicked up.

"Are you telling me I should abandon my cause? Do you know what I've seen, uncovered? If I told you—"

"I don't want to know, because I'm not supposed to be involved. But I can imagine. I've seen some pretty awful stuff too. We're trained for that, or at least try to be. You're a civilian. Don't underestimate the effects of fear on the human body. Sometimes long-time criminals who get away get tired of looking over their shoulders and commit a crime just to be caught so they don't have to live with the uncertainty of it. It takes lots of training to not allow your fears to make choices that might not be in your best interest. Think about that, Kiley."

"I can handle it."

But she could see he wasn't convinced, and that bothered her. Maybe he didn't believe in her abilities to finish her mission.

"Don't you think I'm strong enough to deal with it?" she asked.

"How can you prepare for something you don't completely understand? Did it occur to you that what you've stumbled upon is bigger than it appears on the surface? What if you've hit a hornet's nest? Make sure you're not spinning a fairy tale, Kiley. Very dangerous to underestimate the enemy. And it comes at you when you least expect it."

"Now you sound like my editor. Although at first, he didn't believe a word I was saying."

"I believe you, Kiley. But I'm not sure you're seeing

the big picture. You didn't sign on as a detective, and you have no training in that. These guys do this sort of thing all the time, and even they miss stuff. They get blindsided by things out of their control. And they're trained to look in all the right places. You could have stumbled onto something like that."

"You're scaring me, Jason."

"Good. I think you should take on a heavy dose of reality. Not fear, but the reality of the situation."

She winced. The more they talked about it, the worse she felt.

"Kiley, let's just wait to see what happens with the story. Maybe you're right. Maybe shining the light on their activities will cause other wheels to grind into motion and the authorities can do the rest, like you hoped. But it takes more than hope and determination to come up against these guys."

She finished her coffee, frowned and handed him the mug.

"I think you worry too much, Jason. I must have just forgotten where I was. That must have caused the dream. You're acting like I have some form of latent trauma, which is ridiculous. I'm going to take a shower."

The warm water completed the job of bringing her back to life. She thought about the other SEALs she met last night and the women who were with them. She had expected to hear war stories, but all they talked about were the practical jokes they played on each other all the time and the things they did while they were waiting. Lots of waiting. It was a surprise to learn that was their biggest complaint, to be all geared up and ready only to have to wait and hope that their timing wasn't off.

She told them a little about what she'd been doing, trying to expose abuses going on in women's shelters and how young women and children were being smuggled into the city and used for sex. She'd uncovered a network of City-sponsored women's shelters that were fronts for what looked to her like organized crime enterprises. That's when the team guys got silent. The questions stopped and she hesitated to go into much more detail. She saw their eyes travel from her face to Jason's. Some kind of signal was given.

"You're naming names in this article of yours?" finally asked Cory.

"Some, yes."

Corey returned her comment with a whistle. Jason's former teammate, Andy, made a point of telling her he hoped she was taking precautions and that she should be very careful.

"Hell, I'd just stay here," Cory answered.

The conversation ended. After they'd consumed all the beer, Andy handed Jason a guitar and asked him to sing.

As the water continued sluicing down her body, she remembered Jason holding the guitar with reverence. She remembered how his magic fingers toyed and tuned the strings just like he'd played her body. He closed his eyes and began singing old favorite Hawaiian songs, his voice lilting and full of passion. Into the firelight, he sang his gift that soared to the heavens with the fingerlings of fire.

As she dried off, she remembered the hush that came over the group and his peaceful smile as he dedicated a Hawaiian love song to Kiley he refused to translate.

When she walked into the bedroom to gather her clothes, Jason was on his phone. He hung up, a somber expression taking over his face.

"Bad news?" she asked.

"I'm afraid so. I've got orders to report back to Coronado."

"Just you?"

"No, Damon and another guy here from our Team. We're to catch a flight tomorrow around noon. So this is our last night here."

She was crestfallen. There was so little time. So much had not been said.

"So what does that mean?"

"Well, it means we're going to get together tonight, like we planned. But it will have to be an early night. Then I've got to leave you, Kiley."

"How long will you be gone?"

"Can't say, and we really never know." He shook

his right shoulder. "They'll have all the details worked out by the time we get to California tomorrow. We could fly out right away, or it could be hurry up and wait."

"Is this how it always is?"

"More and more, yes. We're called as needed. Stuff happens. It never happens on schedule."

He watched her get dressed. She could tell he wanted to say something but was holding back. Then he whispered, "I'm so sorry, Kiley. I truly am."

It sounded more like a final good-bye than a good-bye for now. Her stomach began to burn. She was fighting inside—fighting something she would have to accept later. This untimely mission might mean that the relationship which had begun between them would forever be dashed, never given a chance to grow and develop into something she was sure would be beautiful and everlasting. But was this her imagination running wild again? Was he right? Was she chasing windmills and trying to do things that were impossible? Was any of this real?

His face was without emotion. A mask had covered what was once there.

Unsure whether or not it was her right to ask, she decided to pose her question.

"Will I see you again?"

"Of course. Sort of depends on you, though," he

said.

"How do you mean?"

Jason's face was hard to read. "We've had a nice time together. Kind of took me by surprise, to be honest. I normally don't do this sort of thing," he said.

"What sort of thing?"

"Jump in fast. Play house on the first date, that sort of thing. Maybe I've been unfair to you. I'd like to stay in touch, but I have no expectations, nor do I have any claim on you, Kiley. You're here, in Florida, but your real life's in Portland. My life's in Coronado, and it has to remain that way. I expected we'd have some time to talk, you know. Get to know each other more, but—"

"We've talked," she joked, trying to keep it light-hearted, but her insides were shredded. She hoped her mask was holding up as well as his was.

"Yeah, we did." He looked down at her with a grin that sent sizzles down her spine.

She knew he was right. They'd jumped in so deep without knowing anything about each other, and now separating so soon felt like the end of a beautiful dream. It was going to be hard to concentrate, thinking about what a wonderful time they'd had. It was more than sex for her. She was going to miss him for reasons she couldn't work out yet. She just knew it was going to be the case.

"You didn't get to see the best part of Florida," she finally said.

He studied her body slowly, the grin deepening. "I think I saw all the best parts of Florida. Those are places I'd like to return to, some day, when the time is right."

"So would I, Jason. Is it wrong for me to want to see you again? After I get home, can you visit me up there?" A tiny slip of fear cooled her veins. She didn't want to hold on too tightly. She could scare him away.

"You're still thinking about going back to Portland?"

"I can't stay here forever."

Jason looked through the window to the beach and waves beyond. "There are worse places to be. It's kinda grown on me. But I understand. Hawaii will always be my true home, too."

She walked to the sliding glass door, looking out at the ocean. She didn't want this to end, but she was a grown up. The best thing she could do right now was to show him that. Besides, there had never been any promises made, like Jason said. Their worlds were so far apart it was hard to imagine they could stay connected, as nice as it felt to think about it that way.

"Come on. Let's take a walk," he urged.

He took her hand, and they made their way down to the surf. Kids were digging in the sand, creating forts and collecting shells. Couples of various ages walked slowly by. The bicycle crowd was missing today, but a group of women runners greeted them. It was almost painful for her to see normal life breezing by, seemingly carefree, while she was carrying such a heavy burden, knowing that she was going to have to let go of something she wasn't ready to release. She was going to miss him.

Barefoot, they let the water lap at their feet. The full noonday sun wasn't out yet. He pulled her hand and they walked along the shore.

"Tell me about Hawaii?" she asked, thinking it might be the last time they could talk about it.

"Hard to describe how I feel about her. Whenever I think of home, I smell flowers, I see dancing, family get-togethers, the little kids running around, barbequed pig and fresh fruit. Hawaii is like a beautiful woman with a perfect body, who will never grow old. The sunsets are like here."

"Sounds beautiful."

"People come from all over the world. We used to say in high school that Hawaii always breaks everyone's hearts. They want to come back, but most never do. I guess that's like here," he said.

Kiley didn't agree. "No, you're wrong. People come here to heal. I have this plaque at my place—"

"I've seen it. The beach heals everything."

"Yes. That's the way it is. There's a part of me that never wants to leave. Yes, I've carved out a place in Portland, but when I'm done saving the world, maybe I'll come back here and just heal."

"That's when you'll fall in love, Kiley."

The comment disturbed her. He was slipping away

right in front of her and there wasn't anything she could do about it. And then his final thought drove the final wedge into her heart.

"When your work is done, you'll find someone on a beach just like this. And you'll set down roots. I'll go home to Hawaii and pick myself a nice island girl and make lots of *keiki*, kids."

She turned so he wouldn't see her tears. Mustering all the strength she could find, she bravely continued, trying not to let her voice waver.

"After you're done saving the world."

He nodded, "Yes, after I'm done."

The timing of all this sucked. Why couldn't they have met in a different time. Maybe same place, but different time.

"So why did you say it was up to me?"

He led her to sit on the sand several feet from the surf.

He kissed her hand. "When you're done battling those demons in Portland, if you come back here, maybe I'll join you. But only after you're done. And only after I'm done."

What was he saying? Was there hope, still? Taking a deep breath, she stopped short. She didn't have words to answer him.

"Don't make promises you can't keep, Kiley." He faced the ocean, but his hand still held hers. He rubbed his thumb over her knuckles.

Was he asking that she give up her dream? Did he

mean she should stop defending the helpless victims of these predators and creeps?

"But you would give up being a SEAL? You would consider getting out?"

"I didn't say that. Not yet. The work isn't done. I have a contract to fulfill. I made a vow and I'll not go back on that word. But there's always life after. And I won't fight someone else's war. I do what I'm signed up to do. I don't make the fights."

She wasn't sure she fully understood him. So she asked.

His answer surprised her.

"It's hard enough being with someone. Impossible if their battle and inspiration is elsewhere. If I put my Trident away, I want only one thing to focus on, one project left to accomplish. And for that, I'd give the rest of my life."

SHE WATCHED JASON all evening as he laughed, drank beer and savored the buttery crab they'd all been looking forward to. They told more silly stories. He demonstrated part of a Haka, a fierce Maorian dance he'd learned growing up. The patterns on his chest and arms seemed to come to life as he danced. Andy and Damon even joined him, playing the comic relief, unable to even partially imitate all Jason's moves. He stretched his neck, stuck out his tongue and puffed up his chest, his enormous hands balled into fists he'd slap against his thighs. He was twice the size of anyone else in the restaurant.

With twice the heart.

She met Madison, introduced as Ned's girl. Her mother was right in the middle of the conversation, along with her salty pirate boyfriend with a patch.

If they'd had more time, she would have participated more. But tonight she wanted to watch him, absorb everything about him so she wouldn't forget a single smile, laugh, or glance back in her direction.

And the more she watched, the greater her heartache.

Later, when they returned to her place, she found it difficult not to cry as he softly worshiped her body for the last time. He chuckled, trying to console her, pretending that she was being silly. But he knew. He just covered up that part of him better. She was certain he would miss her too. She'd touched his heart and he had fed hers.

She was going to crave him forever.

Kiley had told herself she'd get up and kiss him good-bye, but when she awoke, he was already gone. On the kitchen table, he left a note with a bright fuchsia flower on top of it. He just signed his name and wrote his cell number.

CHAPTER 9

JASON LET ANDY and Damon imitate his dancing from last night while they waited for their plane in Tampa. He didn't mind the joking around, because it took his mind off of things he had no right to think about. Unwelcome thoughts and anxiety over flying left him grateful for their antics. They'd waited in line to turn their cars in, waited in line to board the plane. Sat in crowded seats until they were upgraded to First Class. He drank a beer, hoping it would help him sleep, but fussed, napping off and on all the way back to San Diego.

He tried not to think about Kiley, but it was impossible. He'd done the right thing to not encourage her too much, but he still felt bad about it. It felt dishonest. Was he doing it for her, or for himself? If she'd have asked him, perhaps he would have just junked his whole career and disappeared with her. But that wasn't really who he was. And she was woman enough not to ask that of him. But it still hurt.

Everything else around him was just noise. He hitched a ride to where he'd left his truck, grabbed clean clothes and his gear after a quick trip to his apartment, and headed back to the SEAL Team 3 building where they'd discover the details of their mission.

He could always tell the importance of the mission by the number of cars in the lot. Today, it was packed.

His team didn't always go out together, often divided up into squads, depending on the action and the talent they required. Sometimes they'd employ other Special Forces talent on loan from other branches or specialists from the CIA or State. The group who stood up front with Kyle had some new faces.

But two of the faces he recognized were Kelly Fielding and Sven Tolar. He'd not been on the op when Team 3 had rescued Kelly's sister in the Canaries, but Sven had been a regular at the Team building, working out with the guys. Jason had sat in while he talked about his FSK days as part of the Norwegian Special Forces group. Jason knew him to be a fierce warrior.

Jason received thanks from several brothers for carrying Thomas home. A couple of training buddies were there, as well as several men he'd gone through BUD/S with who had been medically rolled and graduated in later classes. Several asked about Andy, and Jason relayed the good news of his transfer and remarks about the new house they were working on at Sunset Beach.

He sat down with Ned and Damon. T.J. Talbot joined them, as well as several others from the previous missions.

Kyle Lansdowne began his address to the group of approximately sixty SEALs from Team 3.

"Welcome, gentlemen. We've assembled a rather large group here today, as I'm sure you've noticed. Most of you know everyone on board, but we have a few froglets here, so let me introduce you to the team."

"We have Lt. Commander Andrew Gibson, who led one of the previous forays this mission is a follow-up to."

Gibson stepped forward and waved. "Glad to be with you, fellas."

"He is joined by Lt. Jack Gridley, who has not only recovered from his honeymoon the last time, but now has a bouncing baby boy at home. That means she forgave him enough to have sex with him at least once."

The men laughed. Gridley turned bright red from the attention. Although an officer and former cop, the Lt. looked barely old enough to be out of high school. He was a by-the-book officer, not quite sure of himself. That's why the team liked to needle him so much.

Gridley had learned one thing that would lead to a successful Naval career: let them do it, as long as they didn't push too far.

"So his wife wants you guys to be really careful with his person, if you know what I mean," Lansdowne continued. "Apparently, she's not done with him yet."

The group chuckled again. Trace and Tucker riddled him more than others.

"Are you sleeping in separate beds yet?" Tucker asked.

Trace added, "I'm more interested in the naked penance you had to do as you begged for forgiveness to keep your marriage intact."

Gridley appeared to be a good sport. "Only for you, Trace. We're hoping not to have to make a do-over. If we do, we'll re-do our vows, unlike others I know here."

Jason knew the two older SEALs on the Team were much revered. Both had been involved in messy first marriages and were happily married the second time around. Trace married Tyler's wife's older sister, Gretchen, and was fathering her three girls from her first marriage to the former NBA star Tony Sanders.

Gibson was a good Commander, mostly because he trusted his enlisted men and rarely overruled them. He didn't brag and rarely showed off. He liked to joke but kept his opinions about anything controversial to himself. Jason felt lucky to be under his command.

Lt. Gridley was also well liked, his confidence growing with each successful mission he was part of. In the field, he stuck to Kyle Lansdowne like glue.

Kyle introduced Sven Tolar and Kelly Fielding, who were on special assignment from the State Department.

"We're going back to the Canaries." The lights dimmed and pictures flicked on from the last mission there, including pictures of two associates of the now-deceased gun-running billionaire Lars VanValle—Nigerian warlord General Two Fingers, and Jens Vandershoot, both captured on the previous trip but subsequently released.

"We don't yet have all the details, but have reason to believe they are back in operation, being funded by their benefactor's heirs, who now run the cartel from Europe. They have a fleet of cruise ships they've recently purchased on the open market from a now-defunct Italian cruise line, and are operating them as floating brothels."

Kelly Fielding stepped next to Kyle and interrupted, "If I may?"

Lansdowne nodded.

"They are learning. We have intel that says they have sold shares in these ships, "condominiumized" them, so to speak, using some Dutch loopholes in maritime law. That makes this a legal enterprise. In short, they've gotten quite blatant, giving partial title to these floating palaces, even registering them such that wealthy businessmen can claim a tax deduction and write off the expenses as legitimate costs. What is illegal, however, is the trafficking of young men and women, who are conscripted for sex and the chance of a better life amongst the rich and powerful."

The room was deadly silent. Jason knew this sort of crime, the selling of human flesh, was on the top of their team's most hated list. Variations of the same themes had been operating for centuries and had touched just about every country in the world.

His grandmother told him stories of how early slaves had first made it to the Hawaiian Islands from the Orient, and that some of his ancestors had borne some of that guilt.

His LPO continued the logistics, how the team would be flown over and what the squad breakdown would be. They were to leave at 0800 for the flight to New York and then on to Gran Canaria via a stopover and plane change in Madrid. Jason calculated the flight times and discovered it would take them over thirty hours to reach their destination.

He hated long flights almost as much as he hated long airport waits. He'd be exposed to both this time around.

He made plans to have an early dinner with Ned and Damon, plus a couple others on the team before returning home to re-pack and get to bed at a decent time. He knew better than to be able to count on getting any sleep on the planes, since flying made him nervous.

On their way over to the Rusty Scupper, Jason dialed Kiley and was pleased she picked up right away.

"Africa? I didn't know we had troops in Africa," she said.

"Well, not exactly a deployment of troops. Just a mission. And that's an approximate. I can tell you more when I return. But I thought you'd worry less if you knew it wasn't somewhere in the Middle East," Jason said, even knowing there really was no completely safe place to be. The places that looked quiet and normal were some of the deadliest. Africa was in some ways more dangerous. But she wouldn't suspect that.

"You've got that right. So when do you leave?"

"Tomorrow. Early. So this will have to be good-bye for now."

"For now. That's how you say it."

"That's how we say it. I didn't get to mention some things you need to know. You can't just call me, Kiley. I mean, I won't pick up. I will call you. My phone's shut off as soon as we take off. It might take me days to see a message from you. But it doesn't mean I don't care, okay?"

"I got it."

"I'm going to send you my LPO's wife's contact information, so if there's anything that comes up and it's like an emergency, you can call Christy."

"LPO?"

"Leading Petty Officer. He's sort of my direct boss, Kyle. You can ask Aimee about it. She's met them both. If you have any questions, talk to her, okay?"

"I will. I was going to see Aimee tomorrow. She and Andy wanted to take me shopping, distract me, or so they said."

"I think it's a good idea. Stay close to them, at least until Andy's gone. And just as an aside, stay away from Cory."

"Why?"

"Just do it, okay? If you're going to hear any horror stories, I want to be the one to tell you."

"Fair enough."

Jason knew she wanted to ask more questions so he offered help. "What else do you want to know?"

"How long will you be gone?"

"Depends. We really don't know."

"Will you stay in San Diego long after you get back, or will you come back out to Florida? Or maybe stopover in Virginia, maybe you could come down for a visit? Is that in the cards?"

"Kiley, I wish I could say. Everything's up in the air. Best not plan on anything. But I'll do what I can to be in contact. Sometimes we can facetime, but no guarantees."

"Can I write?"

"I'll read it when I get back. Writing's good."

"What if—?"

He knew what she wanted to know. "If anything happens to me, you'll be contacted. That's not going to happen, though. The best thing you can do is just go about your life. Focus on what's happening in Portland. And I still think you should contact the Pinellas County Sheriff. I would feel much relieved if you did that, Kiley. Don't try to do this alone."

Jason pulled up to the restaurant next to Damon's truck. He waved, showing he was still on the phone. Damon went inside.

Kiley whispered, "You forget, they don't know how to find me. I'm small potatoes, Jason. All I did was knock the hornet's nest around a bit. Besides, Carmen doesn't even know for sure where I am. I'll get a good feel for what's going on when I call her today. Perhaps it will spur an investigation, maybe even a grand jury probe. That's what we're hoping for."

"I still think it's foolish not to involve the local law enforcement guys. But, hey, I don't want to use up our time talking about it. Just be careful and know that I'll be thinking about you nearly twenty-four seven. That's a promise."

"I can make the same promise, Jason. And I'm going to say the same thing you told me. Don't worry, okay?"

He chuckled. "Fair enough." He didn't know how to end the call. He decided to give advice he'd once heard someone else give. "Stay busy and stay with other people in our community. That way, the time goes by faster. Don't find yourself alone. Stay with friends, people we know. Be social, connected. Don't try to do this on your own."

"Thank you. But I still am going to miss you."

"You better. I'm counting on you being able to show me when I get back. Be safe, Kiley."

He wanted to say more, but the timing wasn't right. And he'd not practiced that part enough. This was all new territory. He'd never left for a mission with someone like Kiley behind.

"Jason, I know you're doing something good for the world. I'm proud of you. So, go save the day, or something like that."

"That was perfect. Be safe, Kiley. I'll call you when I can. Miss you."

"Miss you more. And about the calling, I'll be getting a new number, so I'll leave you a message when I do. And I still miss you more."

"Impossible. Sweet dreams."

He hung up because they easily could have spent an hour saying good-bye. He knew something new was brewing. It was like the panther his grandmother had talked about, lurking in the jungle. He'd been so afraid when she'd told him the stories he couldn't sleep for two days. Even though she told him panthers didn't live in Hawaii, he didn't believe her.

He now knew what she'd been trying to tell him. She wanted him to keep an eye out for danger, lurking where it was least visible. Hiding somewhere ready to pounce.

Jason knew he couldn't control the circumstance, but he could stand ready. He could call on the chanting of his ancestors to ward off the evil panthers lurking in the jungle, while he transformed like the ancient warriors centuries ago.

He knew exactly what this new transformation was. The goddess of love had captured his heart and was holding him hostage. Like a tricky panther, he'd use it to spur him on to pay attention.

There was now more to live for.

CHAPTER 10

Aimee and Martel took Kiley shopping where she bought two more cheap prepaid cell phones and some groceries. They visited a bookstore Martel wanted to check out. Aimee stopped by a local hardware store and picked up paint she'd ordered, along with some painter's tape and extra rollers. Afterward, they had lunch together at a tiny brewhouse down by the beach.

Breathing in the fresh gulf air was the best medicine in the world for Kiley. Today was windy, and several large dragon kites were flying high, soaring and diving in the fall wind.

"Are your guys nervous?" Aimee asked.

Martel shrugged. "I can never tell anymore. It's like they train them how to talk to us. You couldn't get a thing out of them they don't want to tell us. But he did tell me Africa."

"That's what Jason said too." Kiley was enjoying

the camaraderie with the two SEAL wives. "Are you going out to San Diego at Christmas break, Martel?" she asked.

"Yup. I'm taking an extra week, so I'll be there almost a month. I'm hoping to spend enough time there to get pregnant. That's the plan, anyway."

"Oh! That's exciting!" said Aimee. "But aren't you going to stay teaching here?"

Martel smiled. "I think so. But if the timing works, I might be able to take maternity leave and have the baby in San Diego, which would be way better. We'll only have a year left on his enlistment after that, so we'll see."

Kiley asked, "Why doesn't he transfer to an East Coast team?"

"He might," Martel returned. "If he stays in, he could join Andy maybe on Team 4. Maybe if Jason transfers, too, well, they'd all be together. But we have to wait to see. A lot can happen in the next year plus. First, we gotta get pregnant. I can teach anywhere but I love my school, and this is now more my home than San Diego. But we'll see."

"I guess you have to stay flexible," Kiley added, watching the two kites nearly collide.

Aimee nodded. "Way better than regular Navy where they're stationed all over the world or gone for huge blocks of time. I can't complain, really. As long as

Andy is happy. So far, he's gotten along well with the Team 4 guys he's met."

"When does he start?" Kiley asked.

"Twenty-one days. We've been doing a big push to get the house finished before he has to leave again."

Both the wives looked at Kiley. Martel spoke up first.

"You can ask us anything you want to know, Kiley. Lots of times, the ladies have questions."

Kiley appreciated their kindness but had found herself distracted by the screams from a child who had fallen in the surf and was brought up sputtering by one arm, his mother wrapping him safely in a huge beach towel to quell his sobbing. That also reminded her of the phone call she was going to make to Carmen this afternoon, and her stomach lurched. "I'm not sure we're there yet. What a sweet guy. If only we had more time before he left." She knew it probably wasn't a very good lie, but wasn't going to make all her feeling public. Not yet.

"He's so wonderful, Kiley. Not a big partygoer and just a solid guy. All the Team guys like him," said Aimee.

Martel agreed.

"Well, we've really just met." Kiley hoped they would drop the subject. "Like you, Martel, we'll have to just see how it goes. It's going to be hard to maintain a relationship with someone when we're both so dug into our jobs."

"I enjoyed being up there." Martel reached for another French fry and dipped it in catsup. "Portland is a great city. But I can't see a Hawaiian boy living in the dreary rainy winters in Oregon," she added. "Florida would be a much better fit."

"San Diego," said Kiley. "I think that's where he wants to be. He has to be near the beach."

Martel agreed.

Aimee's eyes sparkled. "I think the two of you make a cute couple. I can see you living here. I'm keeping my fingers crossed for both of you," she continued. "I'm hoping Team 4 is in your future! Yours too, Martel."

"Amen to that," Martel said as they toasted their white wine.

Kiley liked the idea more than she wanted to let on.

AIMEE DROVE THEM back to her house where Kiley said her good-byes and walked along the beach until she came to the access path that led to her place. With a persistent wind blowing off the gulf, the beach was sparsely populated. The fat tire motorized bicycle brigade had swollen to four, all of them men and all but one silver-haired, riding their bikes in flip-flops and swimming trunks.

Kiley tried the sliding glass door onto the patio and was reassured to find she'd remembered to lock it before she left. She went around and entered through the front door.

Inside the house, she put away her things and un-boxed one of the cell phones, turning it on. Then she removed the sim card from her old phone, cutting it with scissors and flushing the pieces down the toilet.

She dialed Carmen.

When the reporter's voicemail came on, Kiley left a short message.

"Hey there, it's me. I'll try you at the office. This is my new phone number."

She left a brief message for Jason before she called the paper asking for Carmen.

The receptionist didn't recognize Kiley's voice, which was a lucky break. She was transferred to the features desk, and again, she heard Carmen's voicemail. "Okay, quit playing hard to get, Carmen. I'm here. Waiting for your call."

When she didn't hear from the beat reporter after an hour, she called her editor.

"Kiley, I'm glad you called…just a minute while I close the door."

Corbin Newman's voice was heavily laced with stress. He'd never taken the time to close his door on their prior calls.

"Is everything okay? I was actually calling for Carmen—"

"There's been a development, I'm afraid," he interrupted. His breath sounded constricted and the pitch of his voice was a little higher than normal. She heard fumbling as he'd put the phone to his ear while walking from the office doorway. The familiar squeak of his rolling desk chair told her he was now ensconced behind his desk.

"Tell me, Corbin. What's happened?"

"Carmen's missing."

It took a couple of seconds before Kiley could fully comprehend her editor's words. Something at the back of her brain screamed a denial. Her Aunt Itoldyouso was standing in the distance with her hands on her hips, shaking her head.

"Since when?"

"Since yesterday. I didn't want to call you to worry you further, after our last conversation, but was just going to call you this morning when we still hadn't heard from her. I have Fred and Doris headed over to her place now."

Fred was their head of security. So Newman suspected foul play.

Kiley instinctively scanned the patio and the beach beyond in both directions through the still-locked and closed sliding glass door. Nothing caught her eye. She ran to the front door and double locked the deadbolt and door handle. Her fingers felt clammy, and sweat poured from her armpits. The familiar thump, thump-thump of her elevated heartbeat made her teeth rattle.

"Talk to me, Corbin."

"We're stumped, Kiley."

"So how do you know she's missing, then?"

"She was to do an interview with KRVR. The article hit the papers yesterday—"

"I thought it was coming out Friday."

"We upped it. There was interest, you know, rumors of the article coming out. I can smell a request to cover up news a mile away. KRVR left me a message late yesterday afternoon when she didn't show up for the taping. It was going to be their lead story on the evening news, and the old lady was furious with me, like it was my fault."

The public radio station was owned by the ex-wife of a wealthy Oregon state representative. She ran the station like her own private fiefdom. Kiley could only imagine how Rosalie Conden had boxed his ears. He was probably still sore.

"So what did they say then, on the newscast?"

"Oh, they announced they were doing some investigative reporting on your article, didn't mention anything about Carmen, thank God, and just indicated there would be more coming. Rosalie had her toy-boy do it, the anchor, what's-his-name."

"Charley Gleason."

"That's the one. It made me nervous to look at him deliver his script. It's got me spooked, Kiley. Are you sure you've not heard from her?"

"Positive." Kiley had forgotten to check for messages before she destroyed the sim card, and she swore at her aunt, mentally. "What's the feedback on the article?" She inhaled deep and waited for an answer.

"Oh geez, like a bomb went off. We've been doing nothing but fielding phone tips all morning. I had to hire an extra receptionist to handle the volume. And then there's the mayor. Haven't returned his call yet. I spoke to the chief, briefly, and promised we'd cooperate fully when I located either you or Carmen. He wants a call back from you, especially. They're all talking about it in the bullpen."

"And Martin? I'll bet he's chomping at the bit."

"I haven't seen him."

That gave Kiley an idea. "Go check Carmen's desk. Make sure she didn't leave her story files behind." It had always annoyed Kiley that Newman didn't allow them to lock their files, not that a zero-skilled person couldn't pry open a desk drawer. But there had been accusations of some "lifting of the jewels" as Corbin had phrased it during one office meeting when it came up. His answer was, "Take everything home with you unless you need it locked up in my safe."

He always considered it sheer stupidity if a staffer lost out on a scoop because they'd been careless to leave things so easily accessible.

Newman gave Kiley the cell phone number of Chief Rayburn. Just before they signed off, he barked, "Oh shit. I'm getting a visit from the mayor as we speak. Call me back after you call the chief, okay?"

"But—"

"Just do it, Agnes." His tone changed as Kiley could hear sounds that the door to Corbin's office had opened. In a syrupy-sweet voice he continued, "I'm sure he'll come home by tomorrow. I'll help anyway I can. Um, I have to go now, Agnes. Don't worry. Your cat will come home. You'll see. Bye."

The line disconnected.

Kiley stared into the phone like it was the end of a lifeline that had been cut from her arms. Carmen was missing. Jason was clear across the country or halfway around the world by now. Aimee and Martel were probably still at Aimee's house, making plans to paint one of the bedrooms upstairs. People passed by in the distance, but their images were blurry. Then the outline of the glass door became wavy as she realized tears were streaming down her cheeks and dropping onto her chest.

Her fingers were stiff and cold as if the wind was

blowing through the glass. She touched the warm wetness of her tears on her shirt. How she wished they were tears of joy, how she wished those huge arms of his could grab her, hold her until she stopped shaking.

She'd been grinding her teeth while she was thinking. She'd felt so safe being all the way on the east coast, far away from the dark danger lurking in the streets and alleyways of Portland. She had allies, but none of them were truly available. She considered her options, and as she thought about it, she began to feel better.

I told him I could handle it. That's what I promised. That's exactly what I'll do.

Kiley knew she needed to reach out to Jason. But she didn't want him to worry, because once again, she told herself, *You've got this. You can handle it, Kiley.*

She grabbed her cell and dialed Jason's number again, hopeful he'd pick up, even though he'd told her he wouldn't. After three rings, it went to his voicemail, just like before. The sound of his voice, though canned, still ran her libido around the track and left a deep cavern inside her that hurt as she experienced the reality of the distance between them.

The beep on the message made her jump.

"Jason, this is—" What was she doing? Of course he'd know who it was. "Kiley here. Say, I forgot to tell you I've got some news, and it's not good. But I'm taking charge of the situation. Nothing for you to worry about. If you get a chance, please call me back. I need a little advice. But don't worry."

She hung up, afraid she'd begin to sound emotional. That was the last thing she wanted to show him. But in her haste, she didn't say anything about hoping he landed safely or to stay safe himself. It was all about her.

"Argh!" she screamed as she pulled on her hair.

She toyed with the idea of calling him back and correcting the last message. But that would sound pathetic. She searched her options and came to the conclusion she only had a limited few, and most of them were dangerous.

Then she remembered the phone number to Jason's LPO's wife, Christy. But she hadn't saved the contact information before cutting up the sim card.

Some investigative journalist you are. Losing important information!

The unexpected news about Carmen and everything else had rattled her. She stopped chastising herself and vowed to ask Aimee and Martel later on.

Calm down. All will be well. Keep it together, Kiley. You can do this. You can do this!

Her last remaining piece of hope she spent on one last call to Carmen.

"Please call me back, Carmen. I'm worried about

you. I just need to know where you went and who you talked to. If you can hear this—"

"Hello?" a male voice answered, interrupting the message she was leaving.

"Who is this?" she asked. Her heart leapt to her throat.

"Who is this?" he asked. The voice sounded familiar.

"Martin? Is that you?"

"Kiley. So you're back from vacation then? You sure left a shitstorm here. When are you coming back to the office?"

The coldness returned, freezing her tongue to the roof of her mouth. Her stomach lurched again, this time nearly making her heave. She didn't have any answers for him. She. Had. Questions.

Sucking it up, she forged ahead, "How did you get Carmen's cell phone? And does Newman know about this?"

"I'm at her place now. I'm with Fred and Doris. Well, I was here already, but they've just arrived. Say, we're real worried about—"

"You broke into Carmen's house?"

"She left the back door open. It wasn't hard. Kiley, are you back from Florida? There are so many people who want to talk to you."

"No. But I'm coming."

"That's good. I think that's really good. Fred's calling the police. He's found something—"

The line went dead.

Again, she stared at the keypad, once again cut off from—from a friend. An ally? Or did Martin have something to do with Carmen's disappearance since he hadn't reported in? Maybe he'd taken Carmen's notes.

She was running out of people to trust. Martin knew about her being in Florida, like Carmen said. Everyone knew.

Kiley remembered what Jason had told her, "Stay busy. Stay with people in our community." Maybe it was time to include Aimee, Martel, and Andy in what was going on in Portland, fully brief them before she returned there. Her editor had been right. *Someone* needed to know where she was and what she was doing. Someone who could do something about it. By default, that would be Andy and the girls.

But first, she dialed the number Newman had given her for Chief of Police Rayburn and left her message.

"This is Kiley Worthington, investigative reporter for the *Columbia Passage*. My editor has told me you want to speak to me. I will be flying back to Portland tomorrow, and I'd be happy to answer any of your questions when I get there. I'll check in with you when I land. Thank you, and I hope we can work together to help clean up a couple of things I've uncovered in the course of my investigation. I'll explain everything when I see you tomorrow or whenever. Thanks. Bye."

She quickly made online reservations for a direct flight from Tampa to Portland, paying an enormous amount for the ticket. She'd call her landlady tonight and see if she could get an extension on her stay or some sort of early cancellation discount. If that didn't work out, she figured she could always stay with either Martel or Aimee when, and not if, she returned to the gulf. She'd ask them later on this afternoon.

By tomorrow, she'd be in Portland, and she'd start facing her fears head-on. She'd share her notes with the police, hopefully retaining the anonymity of her sources, and help them find those ten girls and wherever Carmen was holed up. She knew those notes held the answers they needed to complete the mission. Maybe Carmen was just in hiding, keeping herself safely stowed away from harm. She hoped that was the case, though unlikely.

Part of her was excited for this new adventure. The rest of her was filled with the physical pain of missing Jason, almost like an addiction. But it didn't stem from fear. It came from somewhere else. He'd instilled in her the confidence to quit running and start crashing through the waves like one of those rubber boats he talked about. With Jason on her side, the odds were in her favor.

You got this, remember?

She knew he'd be proud of how she was handling things.

CHAPTER 11

THE ENTIRE TEAM took the State Department passenger plane to JFK Airport, but from there they were split into three groups of roughly twenty men. Jason was glad he was traveling with Damon, T.J., Coop, and Kyle. Sven was also to be on their hop to Gran Canaria. Each airline took a slightly different route, but they all had only one stopover. Flight times ranged from seventeen to nineteen hours in length. This was the grueling part for Jason.

As luck would have it, they barely had enough time to grab a quick bite to eat before their plane began boarding. The others would be close behind, within a few hours. Several First-Class tickets were available, and the Team opted to give Jason one of them, due to his size. Tucker Hudson scored the other, for the same reason.

The "old man," as they called Tucker, was easy to get along with. Nearly as big as Jason, he was firmly packed and could have done professional wrestling, he was so fit. His run times beat almost everyone on the squad. Jason respected his quiet demeanor, especially under fire.

"How's the little one, Tucker?" The older SEAL was starting all over again, at over forty years of age.

The plane had leveled off, and they'd just been served their drinks.

"Kimberly's getting huge. Almost walking now."

"No shit?"

"I know. Time has just flown by. Seems just last week she was born. She's a strong kid. Got tree stumps for legs and, man, can those little legs kick."

"I'll bet," chuckled Jason. "I'd expect nothing less."

"Some of Brandy's friends have boys that are dwarfed compared to her. We're always trying to be so careful she won't fall on one of the kids in her play-group. I think she's twice their size."

"I'll bet Brandy's happy being a mom."

"Oh yes. She's already got her waitlisted on two preschools and has signed up for baby swim and baby gymnastics. Personally, I think it's a bit much, but Brandy was always a big gal, you know, and she doesn't want Kimberly to not know how to move her body. She wants her to be graceful, if you catch my drift."

Jason knew if he had a daughter some of the same issues would come up. "Daikon legs, they say in the

Islands."

Tucker squinted at him a bit and then decided not to explore the term further.

"Whatever. But I doubt she'll be a ballet star," Tucker said, finishing off his drink.

The thought of having a daughter born with huge calves and "cankles" had never entered his mind before. "She's just probably self-conscious. See, in my culture, being big was actually something that was highly prized. The girls were beautiful when they were young, but our women get bulky fast."

"Yea, but they could beat the shit out of anyone who messed with their kids, I'll bet."

Jason nodded. "Very true."

They were served another scotch.

Tucker leaned over and whispered, "Frankly, they should just leave us the tray of little bottles. Everyone else is having wine or beer."

"I'll see what I can do. It is a shame to waste all that booze, isn't it?"

"Damn straight," Tucker grumbled.

"Funny how some people worry about body image so much. In my family, the men got skinny and small and the women got huge. Kind of a role reversal thing," Jason told his buddy.

"Women are more highly prized in your culture, then?"

"It depends. I think it's more about size than gender. I had two Samoan sisters who used to beat the crap out of me every chance they could get. My dad and grandfather thought it was funny, and it wasn't, really. Grandpa would whisper to me, 'Hit her back,' and I never could for fear my grandmother would cast a spell on me. They did it because they outweighed me by double."

"That can't have been very good for your ego," Tucker barked. "So, what did you do, or did you live continuously in fear?"

"One day, I hit her back. She, the older one, had a black eye that nearly extended from her unibrow down to her jaw. Big and purple. Looked like a birthmark. And with her bloodshot eye, she looked like a witch in a Disney movie. My dad was worried we'd have to leave the island."

Tucker found that funny and belly-laughed for several minutes. "There's something so pure about that, Jason. A bully is just a bully when it comes down to it. That was justice. You're a force for good."

"I spent half the year mowing the family's lawn, too with one of those push mowers as my penance. They'd sprinkle the grass with dog poop from the neighbors."

Tucker was losing it, but Jason had never considered it a funny story.

"Did they ever outgrow their obsession to torture

you?"

"When I outgrew them. They were still tilting some three hundred pounds at barely sixteen, but I got to be six foot my Freshman year in high school and that kind of ended their fun. Plus, I could way outrun them."

Tucker shook his head, still guffawing from time to time, until the urge left him.

"So were you not closer to your mom than your dad? For some reason, I thought you would be."

"I think I was. Dad was not comfortable around kids. He loved us, but he was more westernized. Worked in a big hotel and had ridiculous hours. Mom and her sisters were the keepers of the stories. I seemed to cleave to that side of things. I was always fascinated with the pageantry of the feasts, the dancing. I started getting my tats at about eleven."

"Whoa! That's not something I could have done. My mom would have shredded my skin with sandpaper if I'd done that."

"Only thing important to my mom was that it looked good. We were starting to experiment on ourselves, and, well, you know, we didn't know what the hell we were doing. And, it's permanent, you know."

"Fuck yeah. I could see how it would be kind of important. I had my ex's name altered, and I can tell you it's not an easy thing to do."

"You shed blood for Brandy. That's a good man!"

Tucker roared at that one, and they clinked their plastic glasses and demanded more. The skinny male attendant did leave them the rest of the tray this time.

"I'm going to sleep through dinner, I think," said Tucker.

"Breakfast. We got breakfast coming, not dinner. And not for another four hours, Tucker."

"Well, if I pass out, wake me, okay?"

"Roger that, buddy."

Jason knew he was going to have to pee, so decided to do it now before Tucker got too comfortable.

"That's a good idea, son," Tucker said as he followed him to the restroom compartment ahead of them.

Jason could hardly fit inside the doorway of the little room. He wasn't sure Tucker would be able to.

He washed his hands and waved to the rest of the squad sitting in the back of the plane then took his seat. He checked his phone and saw the message from Kiley, but was unable to play it. He saved the number to her contact and hoped he'd had enough alcohol in his system for the long nap he desperately needed. But that depended on whether his bladder would let him.

JASON WOKE UP as the plane lurched forward on their ascent. The force of his body against the strength of the seat belt popped the device open and he hit his forehead on the seat in front of him. If Tucker hadn't been seated next to him, he'd have been sprawled on the floor in the aisle.

Tucker's quick hands yanked his shoulders back so his body didn't rise en route to a short flight into the attendant cabin.

"You all right?" he shouted over the noise of the engines.

Jason checked his shoulder, then his chest and held up the broken seat belt with his left hand. "That's never happened to me before."

"Me neither."

Jason had gotten drunk and sober on the plane, the flight was so long. They had each been served double helpings of breakfast, which helped. They'd passed on the mimosas. So when they deplaned in Madrid, both Tucker and Jason went on a quest for some strong coffee and located a small espresso stand. The rest of the squad hung together in the waiting area for the Iberia prop jet to Gran Canaria.

He excused himself to try calling Kiley, but the phone never picked up, since no answering message had been created. He swore to himself internally when he saw the second voicemail, she'd left him and wished he'd tried to listen to that first.

Her first few words sent him immediately into a

runaway elevator.

'*...but I'm taking charge of the situation. Don't worry.*'

It had the opposite effect on Jason. He hoped he could make contact before they boarded. He paced in front of Tucker and a handful of the guys seated in the waiting area until their flight was called.

This time the plane was packed with tourists. The seats didn't incline, and there was no first class. Both he and Tucker were seated in a middle row seat with college-age kids on either side of them. At first, sleep was impossible due to the banter between the aisle seat and the window inhabitant. Tucker stopped it on his side by growling with his eyes closed. Shortly afterwards, Jason could detect some of Tucker's world class farts, and that seemed to quiet the whole back end of the plane for nearly an hour.

Finally, nearly twenty-four hours after landing in New York, they arrived at Gran Canaria and the port city of Las Palmas. They were shuttled by van to a small resort right on a stretch of pristine beach with a view of the blue waters of the Atlantic in severe contrast to a line of stark white cruise ships.

Kyle and Jack Gridley were to take Kelly Fielding and Sven Tolar and check in with their Spanish liaisons downtown, as well as secure reserved transportation, while the rest of Jason's flight was left to explore the picturesque town nearby with its numerous watering holes and restaurants. The brick streets and bright-colored plaster storefronts looked like a patchwork quilt of different cultures: Portuguese, Spanish, and old Morocco. They were to return before nightfall to connect with the other members arriving on later flights and to go over the plans for the subsequent days.

He walked with a group including Coop, Fredo, Jake, Damon, and the brothers-in-law Tyler and Trace. Several other groups went ahead separately.

Damon left a message for Martel while Jason did the same for Kiley. "They're shopping. I think that's what she said they were going to do. Martel turns her phone off."

"I got a message from Kiley that there's a little wrinkle in her plans. I'm kind of worried about her. I would think she'd want to be available after that, but who knows?"

"I'm sure they're fine. She'll call. We're what? Five hours ahead here?"

"Yup."

"Might be late, but she'll call," reassured Damon.

Jason walked with his hand in his jacket pocket, gripping the cell he hoped would vibrate soon, connecting him to Kiley's world. He wished she'd gone into detail about the concern he heard in her voice, but there wasn't anything he could do but wait.

Worry over Kiley's phone call made it difficult to play the part of a casual tourist. The fact that all the guys were excessively built and inked didn't help either. Their sunglasses matched, being Navy-issue, which was a dumb mistake someone should have caught.

Though they were on an island with miles of beautiful beach rimming the perimeter, it didn't feel anything like Jason's homeland. For one, the foliage was scarce, not because it wouldn't grow but because every stick of wood was harvested and made into fence posts, used to patch a wall, or turned into some small trinket at the tourist stalls. It was cleaner than he remembered Cape Verde had been, and it had more of a European population of visitors, mostly young twenty-somethings in beach attire. Jason's teammates wore too much clothing and didn't smile.

Well, not until they were eating fresh fruit from a street vendor and a local burro peed on Damon's shoe. That started a series of pranks until they found a pork barbeque stand that served ribs, of all things. The dinner was simple. It consisted of ribs, red rice, beans, and pitchers of some local drink made from coconut milk. In fact, Jason couldn't recall seeing a green vegetable anywhere.

The pork was divine, dripping in hot barbeque sauce with chunks of pineapple in it. They ate steamed yams seasoned with cinnamon, brown sugar, and butter for dessert.

The sun was hanging low in the horizon, so the group commandeered two donkey carts and had a race back to their hotel. Dusty and smelling of alcohol, they entered the lobby to a room filled with newly arrived team guys who were tired, cranky, and lacked any sense of humor.

A list of room assignments were given out. Jason and Damon had been placed together, so they headed to the second floor to unpack their minimal load.

"Have you heard anything from Martel?" Jason asked on the way up the stairs. He was taking them two-by-two, the alcohol in his system giving him an extra spring in his step.

"Not yet. I'm sure she'll call tonight. Might be late." Damon unlocked their door and stepped into a huge room with a balcony overlooking the blue Atlantic. "Wow. This is hella better than last trip."

"Well, you forget, this isn't Africa. It's part of Spain," reminded Jason.

"Would you look at that?" Damon said, opening up the sliding glass door to the balcony.

Jason looked out. A gentle warm breeze blew from the ocean. The surf was flaccid but rolled in nearly a half mile. "Damn, if the surf was any bigger, this would be perfect. I'll bet it is during storm season."

"You're probably right. Just look at all the blue water and beach. Does this remind you of Hawaii?"

Jason listened for a minute and then shook his head. "Not a bit. You can barely hear the ocean. There are no palm trees to sit in the shade. No sounds of the women singing, no smell of flowers. In fact, I don't see any green at all."

"You're kidding. You've got the sun, the beach."

Jason sniffed the air. "Actually, it smells of burro pee."

"Shut the fuck up," Damon said as he looked down at his stained pants and leather sandals. I'll wash everything out tonight. Will that suit you, your Highness?"

"As long as you get that sick puppy smell out, I'm good."

Damon leaned against the railing. "You sure this doesn't remind you of Hawaii? It's an island."

"Nope. That hot, dry sun? Hawaii is gentle. This is harsh. You turn into a prune here. Even too hot for swimming."

"Sort of like Florida, then?"

"A lot like Florida but different." Jason picked one of the beds and then unpacked his shaving gear. He leaned against the doorway of the bathroom just as someone whistled from downstairs.

"Showtime!" said Damon, jumping to his feet.

"Listen, if she calls and I'm asleep, I don't care how late it is. Wake me up, okay?"

"Will do, Jason."

They ran downstairs to join the rest of their teammates who were gathering, waiting for instructions.

CHAPTER 12

K ILEY CALLED AHEAD to make sure Aimee and
Martel were still home and then walked the short
distance to the Carr residence. Andy was puttering in
the kitchen, and he directed her to go upstairs to see
the girls.

"Martel talked to Damon. They arrived safely,"
Andy shouted up the stairs after her.

Kiley leaned over the railing. "When was that?"

"They just hung up. About five minutes ago."

"I wonder why Jason hasn't called me?"

Andy shrugged. He held a glass of wine in his right
hand. "Are you staying for dinner?"

"Do you have enough?"

"We've got plenty."

"Okay then. Let me go check in with Aimee."

"Roger that," Andy said and went back to his food
prep.

She found the two girls painting the smaller bedroom a light shade of blue. "Wow! Looks nice, Aimee."

"You think so? I debated. I thought maybe this room would make a nice nursery, if that should happen. But I liked this blue, and it goes with the color of the sky, so I went with it."

Kiley smiled at Martel. "Andy says you got a call from Damon?"

"Yes, he told me they landed safely. He said Jason has been trying to reach you."

Kiley checked her phone. No messages registered there. "I gave him this number to call. I'll give him a try right now. Just a minute."

She ran to the master bedroom, sat on a chair on the deck overlooking the ocean, and dialed Jason's number again. He picked it up on the first ring.

"Hey there. I've been worried—"

Kiley was relieved to hear his voice. "Nothing to be concerned about. I told you that."

"You need to tell me what's going on, Kiley."

"Corbin published my article early, and they've been getting tips pouring into the paper. He's got the police chief calling me, so it looks like we're getting some action."

"That's good news. So what was the complication you talked about? And, honey, don't ever leave a message like that again, okay?"

"Fine. I won't."

"And? The complication?"

"Now Carmen's gone missing."

"What?"

"I'm going to fly back there tomorrow and do some digging. Find out who she talked to. And now since the police are interested, I'll have someone to give my information to. I'm going to help them, Jason."

"Hold it, Kiley. They said you could help them?"

"Well, Corbin said—"

"Did the police say they wanted your help?"

"The chief called my editor; said he had some questions for me. So, I've left him a message and told him I'd answer all his questions tomorrow when I arrive."

"No way, Kiley. You didn't promise to go back to Portland?"

"I think it will be fine now. I have allies. Michael is on the story, so is my editor, and I have the ear of the chief."

"This is the chief you didn't trust to give the information to before?"

"Yes, but that was—"

"The one hired by the mayor you said told your editor to bury the story?"

"Yes, but that was—"

"And you haven't received any reassurances from anyone. You were not even sure you could trust your editor, last I heard."

"But with Carmen out of the picture, who's going to go interview the houses, and the—?"

"What houses, Kiley?"

"The group homes several of these women were staying at. I've got notes, and interview tapes from the staff. If I have to, I'll share these with the chief so he can do his investigation."

"Have any of the girls been found yet?"

Kiley hesitated. "Just the four."

"It's a very bad idea to go back to Portland," he whispered. "Promise me you won't do that, not until I get back home."

"But you said—"

"I said I couldn't interfere. And I can't. But I can keep you safe. Don't you see the problem?"

"Yes, you're halfway around the world."

"Exactly."

"But I gave my word, and besides, everyone's pulling in the same direction. The police are on board. All the research has been done. Now I just have to give them what they need to launch their investigation."

"You're still in danger."

"But that was only until the report was filed. Now that it's out, the public knows. It's like shining a light on it. I think all the pressure was to stop the publication of my report. That's been done. The cat's out of the bag."

"Except you said you needed to help them with their investigation. You honestly think you'll be able to be involved in that? The police don't work that way, Kiley."

"But I have the notes, the interviews."

"Correct. And that puts you in danger."

"Well, I'd just be helping them. All I would do is show them my findings."

"Which was not in the paper. Not all of it, right?"

"Right."

"So it sounds to me that if Carmen were somehow interfered with, someone didn't want that research to go forward."

"But she never had all the information."

"And don't you suppose they know that by now?"

It hadn't occurred to her that Carmen's status, if she was in harm's way, was altered by the fact that the paper published Kiley's article. A wave of ice water filled her veins and caused that familiar shiver down her spine.

"Who has that information, Kiley?"

"I do." She didn't want to admit it, but Jason was right. And then she thought about her phone. "I should at least talk to the police in Portland, though."

"Probably. They'll find you, if you don't."

"Through my cell. I have to get rid of the cell. I gave that number to the chief."

"Look, Kiley. Wait until I get back. Hopefully, it will be just a couple of weeks. We're not expecting to be here long. I'll ask Kyle tomorrow if I can have leave after we return stateside. Then I'll accompany you. But wait until I get that permission, okay?"

"What are you going to tell him?"

"The truth, or what I believe you told me was the truth. The missing girls, especially the new one. We can look the articles up online. I can't break any laws, and I can't interfere with local law enforcement. But I can protect you. We do that all the time. We protect State Department officials, embassies, traveling heads of state."

"Okay. I'll do it. I'll wait here. And I'll get rid of the cell."

"I think that's wise."

Jason's silence made her nervous. "What are you not telling me, Jason?"

"As much as I hate to say it, I think you should tell Andy. I'd like to hear what he has to say about it. Have him call me if he needs to. But let me ask you one question first."

"Okay."

"Were you absolutely certain you were being followed or that the thing with your cat wasn't just some random act of violence? Were you convinced someone was out to scare you off the story or, worse, silence you permanently?"

It was an easy answer. "Yes, Jason, I was. The letters and the phone calls I got at the paper. And I still am, now because of Carmen. There are too many women missing."

"It has to be someone you exposed or partially exposed in your articles. As long as you can still hurt them, you're in danger. If it ever was real, it still is real. Understand?"

"Yes, I do." She was completely deflated.

"When you set up your new voicemail on the new number, don't use your voice for the message. You have to be careful, Kiley. You know this. Let's be smart."

These were going to be the longest two weeks of her life. Things were spinning out of control, just like Jason said. Just when she thought she had a plan, the goalposts changed the game. He was right. Maybe she shouldn't have assumed her plan would work. She started to doubt herself and feel the burden of what she was putting others through.

Aimee opened the slider, poking her head out. "Everything okay?"

Kiley had been staring off to the horizon. She wanted to go home, have a couple glasses of wine in the bathtub, and go to bed early. But there was a job that needed to be done.

Aimee sat down on a wicker chair next to her, propping her feet up on the crosspiece in the railing. The sun was just setting.

"I thought when I was living in Oregon, with all that rain, that perhaps I'd embellished the golden sunset a bit. I figured it couldn't possibly be as bright and beautiful as I remembered as a child. But I was wrong. It's even more stunning than my memories and the colors are even brighter."

"I know. Once you get some of that gulf sun in your hair, on your skin, in your eyes, I think it travels to your soul. You take a little piece of it with you forever. Almost haunts you, doesn't it?" Aimee answered.

She remained quiet until Kiley developed the thoughts and words she wanted to use.

"That was Jason."

"I figured as much."

They were joined by Martel, who announced, "I think we need some wine right about now."

Aimee called after her, "Tell Andy to hold off on dinner a bit. But we'll be down shortly."

"Sure thing." Martel closed the glass behind her and the two women were alone again.

"Is it good news or…?"

"What I came over here for was to tell you guys I decided to go back to Portland. I'll explain more when

Andy's here, because Jason actually told me to make sure I included him."

"You figure it's safer now?"

"Actually, it's not. But I just promised I wouldn't fly back there until Jason could go with me."

"Makes sense."

Martel was back with a bottle of red wine and three glasses. "Your man is not a happy camper and he said if we weren't down there in thirty minutes, he'd eat by himself and we could go out for a burger."

"Oh, Lord." Aimee shook her head. "He's a creature of habit. Likes everything spelled out. He has rules for everything. Stews about most things and stubborn as they come."

"Oh, that's Damon to a T," said Martel as she poured their glasses. "To the magic of Sunset Beach!" They touched glasses after repeating the toast.

"Mmm. That's good," said Kiley. "I could use a little magic right now."

"So you were telling us you wanted to go back to Portland?"

"I called the reporter who was doing work for a followup article, working with my editor, and now she's gone missing. We have officially four missing girls, and now this reporter. But I've uncovered evidence there are many more. Maybe as many as ten."

"A serial killer?" Martel asked.

"No, it's a human trafficking ring. Very organized, in fact, probably professionally managed, and it has important ties to local government. The piece was to hit the paper on Friday, but my editor printed it early. He felt pressure and was afraid he'd be asked to bury the story. But that put Carmen, the staffer we added to the team, in danger, I think. I was having her follow up on some of the interviews I'd done, to see if we could get some quotes and perhaps their cooperation. It's one thing to talk to a reporter anonymously. Quite another to get involved in a corruption scandal. That's where this is all headed."

"Just what did you expect to achieve going back? Didn't you say you lost your cat, and they vandalized your car?"

"Yes. I think those were attempts to warn me. I thought maybe the article would take some of the pressure off, but it looks like Carman may have walked right into it. I'm worried. I wanted to go do some digging in person, see if I could help find her. I know right where to go too."

Martel was puzzled. "I'm not understanding this, Kiley. Like you told us at the bonfire, once everything came out in the paper, wouldn't that begin to shed light on what was going on? You were thinking the public would demand that investigation."

"I did. And I think that will happen. But I can't just

sit here while I've put Carmen in danger."

"Perhaps," Aimee said, her finger pointing to the sky. "You don't know for sure you did."

"Well, yes. I thought we had a couple of days to do a little more research before the final piece was published. And then we could turn over the complete package to the authorities. Now that won't happen. If something's happened to Carmen, it will be my fault."

"Man, you're awfully hard on yourself," said Aimee. "I thought your editor was the one who made the assignments."

"I overruled him. I made him take Carmen. She didn't want it, either. But I got her involved because I thought she'd do a better job interviewing some of the victims I'd located."

"Wait a minute. You found some of the missing girls?"

"I found other girls. Not the missing ones. But I think some of them knew the missing ones."

"How many girls are we talking about, Kiley?" asked Martel.

"I've got tapes on six. Some written material from three more. With very little verification, I could make a case for at least ten girls who have disappeared that we know of. If this criminal enterprise has been operating for many years, then there could be many more. Hundreds, perhaps."

Kiley noted Aimee's pensive stare at the ball of light now melting into the horizon. Within seconds gray streaks formed, the orange and golden yellow clouds were outlined in light purple, and then everything began to fade, going purple and deeper gray. The water on the gulf went from bright azure blue to navy within ten minutes. The pilgrimage to the surf was over and now was reversing, as people made their way back to their homes or cars parked nearby.

The magic was dissipating, and Kiley actually felt sad.

Aimee continued staring at the water as she whispered, "Do you think we're in danger here?"

Before she could answer, Andy slid the glass door wide and jolted them all. "Hey! I got beautiful steaks downstairs, corn on the cob and a killer salad. I'd like some company for all my troubles."

AFTER DINNER, AIMEE began clearing plates. Kiley rose to help her.

"No, you stay put and tell Andy what you started to tell us upstairs. I've got this."

"Thanks, babe," Andy winked.

Martel opened and then began to pour their second bottle of wine of the evening.

"So, Andy, I talked to Jason earlier and he asked that I explain the pickle I'm in. He said you'd have some good advice."

"Okay, shoot," said Andy.

"Darn, I didn't bring my computer. I shouldn't have left it at the house, either. That was totally dumb of me."

"I've got a laptop. Can you log in on mine?"

"I can try."

"No, Andy, you have all that encrypted stuff. You don't want to mix this stuff with your SEAL things." Aimee pointed to the ceiling. "Martel, go get my laptop on the side table upstairs on my side of the bed."

Martel took the stairs two at a time, her long graceful legs digging into the polished wood with her toes. She returned not more than a couple of minutes later.

Aimee dried her hands and opened the computer to a guest icon. "Here you go. Log in with Safari, or do you use Chrome?"

"Chrome."

"There. Now put your passwords in and we'll delete everything when you're done."

Kiley found her portal at the paper and called up the four articles on human trafficking, dragging them to the four corners of the screen so Andy could read them all. She proofread her last article and was mortified to find a couple of typos.

Andy was able to read and summarize at the same time. "So you were looking into the case of an immigrant girl from Central America smuggled across the border by Coyotes. She traveled with a group of three other young girls, all ranging in ages from ten to fourteen."

Andy read further. "You found they came from the same village, and—their parents wanted them to have a better life in the United States. So, they allowed the four friends to come to the U.S. to work as domestics."

He sat up, frowning. "That's a little young, isn't it? Ten?"

"I was able to contact their parish priest, an American who had been in the Peace Corps and stayed to continue his work there. He said the girls in that village often married before they were fifteen. He told me a man and woman, recruiters, came into the village and looked for girls they could find from poor families, where the parents would appreciate not having to feed one more mouth. And they were compensated." Kiley watched as this sunk into her friend's faces.

"They sold their own children?" Aimee said, covering her mouth.

"Yup."

"Isn't that against the law?" asked Martel.

"It is," started Andy. "But you wouldn't believe the plight of children all over the world, Martel. It's not a safe place for a child. They are bartered for pennies in many areas of Africa, the Orient, even South America.

There are groomers too. People who train them for the slavery they'll be doomed for. Mostly the sex trade. And they get them hooked on drugs, so they won't go far. If they don't know the language and have no papers, once they get to their destination, they owe their entire existence to the people who brought them over. And many don't survive the trip, sadly."

"That's what Jason said. You guys were finding these people in Africa. Is that why he's gone, to look for smugglers?"

"Last two trips have been all about the smugglers. Very dangerous people, Kiley. When you were here, I thought you were talking about some guys who liked to get their jollies having sex with young girls and were kidnapping girls for that purpose. But you're talking about a whole organization. Is that right?"

"I'm afraid so, Andy. If you read on, you can see that there are a number of shelters in the Portland area, funded by some church groups and private businesses, formed to help stem the homeless growth in the area. Originally, they were for unwed mothers, runaways, and girls leaving abusive homes. These houses took care of them until they could successfully get a job and be on their own."

"I don't see anything wrong with that," whispered Martel.

"The city began to give tax breaks to organizations

who ran these. And my guess is that the introduction of the money, brought the crime. All the houses were full all the time, more shelters were needed, and the program expanded. This happened under the radar until people started noticing the girls didn't stay in the area but were shipped all over the United States."

Kiley waited while Andy read on, Aimee looking over his shoulder.

"You did a good job documenting everything, Kiley," Aimee told her.

"I didn't give names. Those I kept confidential, but I have all of them in my files. I interviewed a couple of social workers from Texas who came out to Portland to check on two girls who came through their area and were transferred to one of the shelters. They were unable to locate their girls. I have their pictures. Both of them were twelve, best friends. And it happened the same way. They told us that they came from the same village, and immigration picked them up abandoned by their Coyote in the middle of the desert. They had the address of one shelter with them as their final destination."

"Wow, so someone in Mexico or Central America knew about the place in Portland," said Martel.

"I think so. When the social workers inquired, the house was registered with the State of Oregon under a special license. They were told there were regular inspections, medical and dental services provided, as well as English instruction and skills training. But when they came to check, there wasn't any record of the girls ever having gone through the system."

"How did you get their information, Kiley?" asked Andy.

"They saw my first article in the paper and called me. That led to an interview with the head administrator at the place. I talked to several girls who lived there. It was orderly, clean, just how the social workers had found it earlier in the year. But no one ever remembered seeing the two girls from Guatemala. It was like they disappeared into thin air."

"So you know who's doing this?" asked Andy.

"It goes all the way to the mayor's office. Someone in that office, maybe the mayor himself is either running it, or just making sure it continues to operate. But that's what I put in my article that came out yesterday."

"Way to make friends in high places," Andy whispered. "So you left before this fourth article came out?"

"Yes. I listed the names of the ten girls I knew had been at one of the houses, even recently. And I mentioned the mayor's office. That came out yesterday. I had Carmen following up with another reported missing girl, a domestic helper, and she was reported missing by the wife of a very prominent attorney. An immigration attorney. I checked my records and his name was listed as one of the owners."

"That's an awful lot of coincidences," said Martel.

"My research found that the numbers were increasing, too."

"I agree with Jason. You shouldn't be poking around Portland on your own. I'm off to Team 4 in a couple of weeks. I think you should continue to lie low in Florida. But maybe you should move in with us and let the house go, Kiley."

"I live alone now that Damon's gone," said Martel. "I don't mind the company."

"And there's a couple other things, too, Kiley. We got two guys on the team with Jason who are married to girls from Portland and their families still live there," said Andy.

Kiley was beginning to spring hopeful.

"I'm going to read all this. Why don't you stay the night here, and in the morning, I'll try to put in a call to Kyle and Jason. No promises. But maybe we can plan something out."

"I want to go back to my own bed, Andy. And my computer and other things are there. I shouldn't have left them alone."

Andy stood up. "That settles it. I'm walking you back to your place then. From what you've told us, we can't be too cautious."

CHAPTER 13

THE PICTURE IN the newspaper didn't at all resemble the woman they brought into Natalia's shelter yesterday. Battered about the head with one eye swollen shut and a cut lip, this woman was nearly unconscious, which might have been a blessing. Natalia requested she be seen at an emergency room, but was flatly overruled. Dr. Nash was going to stop by this afternoon sometime, and he was late.

Natalia helped the woman out of her bloody clothes and into her own personal shower because she had installed grab bars. She was no problem to help, since she was very slight, tiny, like a child, almost like all the other ones she'd tended to before. Except this woman, unlike the others, had an education and a job at the same newspaper that published her smiling face. And she wasn't young. It concerned her that there might be a husband or family missing her. Natalia didn't like changes in the routine, because that made her have to think too much.

She laid a clean nightie and a pair of fuzzy socks on the closed toilet lid, with a dark green towel. She knew the drill. Everything the woman touched, even the sheets she slept on, would be burned in the incinerator at the back of the building after she was gone.

She was well paid to not take chances, to clean up the messes and ask no questions. It was the price of what little freedom and autonomy she had. It allowed her to save money, buy things for herself, go to the store to purchase food and pretty clothes, and have the big bedroom with the view of the river. But caring for these orphan women was getting old and Natalia was growing weary of it. Especially with this one so badly beaten up. Natalia wondered if this signaled a change in where they got the girls.

But something else was different about this woman. She spoke English. None of the others she'd tended to had. They came from all over the world, walking into her shelter frightened preteens and walking out into their new lives—lives they'd never dreamed of before— happy. At least, that's what she told herself.

As she checked on the sleeping form of the reporter, she feared the woman's fate might be dangling in Natalia's hands. This woman had been beaten, unlike the others. And that also made her think. She didn't like thinking.

She'd gone to church in Ukraine with her grandmother when she was little. Her babushka taught her how to cross herself, which she now did, reciting the prayer she'd learned. It was one of the only things she remembered about her religion, about her family, about the country she would never see again after she was taken.

From the living room, Natalia heard her two yellow canaries singing in the morning sun. They'd both had a bath and had fresh paper and food in their cages. She sat at the kitchen table, drinking her now-cold tea, and looked down at the newspaper with the smiling picture of the woman whose name was Carmen.

She began to remember her grandmother's house.

Her grandmother's friends told her he was a savior and would take Natalia out of the poverty and hell that was their home. But when she recalled the washed and starched white lace curtains and little yellow birds her grandmother raised and then sold in exchange for extra food or socks for her or some soap or milk, Natalia hadn't thought of that home as living in poverty at all. Sometimes the house was cold and there would be little food, but she didn't starve, and blankets always would warm her.

Her grandmother's loving arms were what she missed most the day the man took her away. Her grandmother was inconsolable, but her friends smiled and told Natalia that it was all for the best.

She would have liked that one last hug. As best she could remember, she was about four years old the day she left.

She'd held the man's hand as he walked her to his warm automobile, a car that drove smooth with music, and a driver with a hat sitting in front. She held his hand all the way to the airport, where fresh clothes were put on her, her hair was braided, and a young lady named Lucy even put pink lipstick on her lips, and then smiled at her handiwork. Natalia didn't like the taste of the bitter substance and wiped it off on her sleeve when the woman looked away.

She climbed metal stairs to a small plane with wide butter-colored leather seats. Lucy strapped her seatbelt on for her and sat across from Natalia while the man smiled and bowed his head and then ignored them both.

She stayed in the man's big house in New York for the first few years, while she learned how to do chores as she grew and was able to assume more and more duties. She was instructed never to play with the other children in the house, who used to make faces at her. She sometimes snuck food off their plates when she cleared the dishes, such delicacies she'd never tasted before.

She asked about her grandmother many times but

never heard anything more about her. In time, she settled into a routine. She became friends with the family dog, Jigs, and would take him for walks around the property, which was gated with armed guards stationed at every entrance she'd ventured to look at. One day, the woman of the house bought a yellow bird, and that became Natalia's fascination and mission in life. She devoted herself to tending to it, changing the paper in its cage. She changed the water twice a day and made sure he never ran out of food. In exchange, he sang the most beautiful songs, just like the birds her grandmother raised.

After the first few months, she would have agreed, if anyone had asked her, that her life was infinitely better than where she'd come from. All her physical needs were met. The young woman who slept in the same room with her wasn't unkind, but she didn't have the same kind of relationship she'd had with her grandmother. Natalia knew she was no longer loved. She was cared for but not loved. And she became satisfied with that.

She felt looked after, useful. She had plenty to eat and warm clothes to wear and a warm bed to sleep in at night. Lucy taught her how to read, since she didn't attend school like the house children did. She took to it voraciously. Her whole world expanded when she could read about fantasy stories from different lands.

She learned about the land of her birth. She learned about America from reading the newspaper every day. Compared to other people's lives, she had to admit she was very, very lucky.

Sometimes the man came into their room at night and would sleep with Lucy. She put her hands over her ears and hid her head under the covers so as not to see or hear anything, because she sensed the man was hurting her roommate. Afterwards, Lucy would cry. Natalia tried to ask her if she was okay, and she was scolded and told to shut up.

And then one night, she chanced a glance over at Lucy's bed and found the man having sex with her from behind, but he was staring straight at Natalia. She froze in place, disturbed with his expression, and then rolled over and tried to sleep. When he left, he whispered something to her, but she didn't listen.

Natalia asked Lucy about the man the next morning when they were doing the laundry, but Lucy slapped her and told her never to bring it up again. Weeks went by without any more visits. Lucy seemed to relax and even started to smile more.

And then one night, he came into the room and visited with Natalia. Nothing was ever the same after that.

Lucy left one spring day, and when she returned with the man, there was another little girl like she'd been once, a brown-skinned girl from Africa who was now about the age Natalia was when she came to the house. Lucy coldly told her that she was going away and that it was now Natalia's job to teach Adoara how to read and write, and do the chores of the house. Doing this and showing her how to take care of the canary for the lady became the two bright spots of the day. The nights were painful and much dreaded. She began wondering if she could run away, perhaps take Adoara with her, since she knew that the cycle would be repeated, and someone else would be brought to the home when she was replaced. And then Adoara would have to bear the man's attentions.

She began to plan, and then a miracle happened. The man was shot by his business partner, or so the newspaper said. She was given a ticket to report to Portland to visit a woman who cared for young orphans, all like her, all without papers. She was told Adoara was placed with another family on the east coast.

Natalia was good at nursing scared children back to health. Many of them came with infections and colds, dirty clothes. She became the big sister to scores of girls who came into the house and then left as they were adopted out.

Except she eventually learned the truth about the adoptions. The girls were sold. Natalia herself knew

that no one would ever want her, so when the opportunity came up to start another home, Natalia was put
in charge. She now had a house of her own to run. She
didn't have to worry about money, food, or her safety.
She had no desire to leave because she was not a legal
resident unless she married someone. The thought of
letting a man touch her ever again was so abhorrent
that marriage was not an option. She didn't feel pretty.
In fact, she felt scared. But the scars were really on the
inside where no one could see. She bore her shame
quietly and the people who came and went, bringing
her the young girls she took care of, all seemed to
understand her circumstances. No one ever reached
out nor was interested.

She felt invisible.

Natalia had followed the stories in the newspaper
about human trafficking and now knew that she, at a
mere twenty-five years old or so, was part of a criminal
enterprise. That could mean deportation if she were
caught. How would she ever survive, or worse, would
she go to jail? So although she knew it was wrong, she
continued working for the men who paid the mortgage
and the expenses, gave her spending money, and most
importantly, left her alone. She didn't drive and had no
bank account so kept everything in cash in a jar in her
snow boots. She had to buy another pair to hold the
next two jars of money she saved. It became a game,

something she did for fun because she had nothing to really spend her money on, but she liked seeing it grow.

She prepared oatmeal for Carmen and went into the bedroom to wake her up.

Carmen could barely sit up. Her eye looked even more inflamed than the day before.

"Where am I?" she asked.

"You're safe. No one's going to hurt you here. I have a doctor coming to give you some medicine. And I brought you oatmeal."

"I don't eat breakfast and I hate oatmeal. I have to get out of here," Carmen said.

"No, that's not possible."

"What do you mean, it's not possible? You can't hold me here." She attempted to get up and then saw the handcuff attaching her ankle to the bed frame.

"It's for your own protection, Carmen." Natalia said. "Here, just try it." She held the bowl of oatmeal out, and Carmen swiped it away, the bowl shattering and sending milk and cereal all over the bed and the carpet.

"You know who I am and you're still keeping me here? That's against the law."

"I don't have the key. Even if I wanted to help you, I can't. They gave me the device here but didn't give me a way to take it off. But these people are not monsters, Carmen. They take—"

"What the hell are you talking about? I'm a free woman! They have no right to do this. And look at my eye, my face." She touched her cheek and winced. "Look what they've done."

Natalia was disturbed by the violence forced upon the reporter. It was never discussed before. She knew with the articles appearing in the paper that something dangerous was brewing. But she kept her calm and didn't let on that she was concerned.

"You have to help me. Call my editor, my friends, please! You are the only person who can help me. I think they're going to kill me."

Natalia thought that was ridiculous. She scowled. "I have worked for these people for several years now. They don't hurt people. They help people."

"They *steal* women. They steal boys too. They kill people. I've learned so much about them. They're dangerous. Trust me, when they are done with you, they'll dispose of you too. They're a bunch of thugs, mobsters. It's a huge ring, and you're helping them."

Natalia wished that she hadn't heard those words. It was so much easier when they didn't speak English.

"I have to clean this up. Your doctor will be here shortly."

"My doctor? You mean the executioner. Please—what's your name?"

"Natalia."

"Listen to me. You're in danger. I don't understand what planet you're from, but when you're no longer young and pretty, they'll have no more use for you."

"I resent that!" Natalia was actually offended. "They've never laid a hand on me, and they don't abuse the girls I've taken care of here at the shelter."

"The shelter. That's a sham. It's a grooming house for foreign prostitutes. They train girls to perform sex for men who like young girls. Boys too. Have you had boys here?"

"Never. No one ever has sex here."

"No, they sell them. They do the bad things somewhere else. But, Natalia, you have to understand, just because you don't see it, surely you understand what's happening. You can't be that stupid!"

She fell back onto the bed and began to cry. Natalia did feel sorry for her. Unlike the other girls, if she somehow had managed to free her, Carmen would be able to fend for herself, get help, and go back to her old life. But of course, that was impossible. She thought perhaps she'd question Dr. Nash when he arrived.

"Give me a phone. I need to call the police. We have to hurry. I have to get out of here."

Natalia looked at Carmen's ankle, now red and slightly bloody from her pulling on it. She didn't have anything strong enough to cut through the chain on the cuffs. She could go to the hardware store and buy some bolt cutters, but if Dr. Nash came by and found Carmen unattended, Natalia knew she'd get in trouble.

And she didn't have a phone. She'd never wanted one before.

"I don't have a phone, Carmen. I don't have anything I can use to remove that device."

"Do you have a neighbor? Someone you could borrow a phone from? Is there a phone booth outside?"

"I don't know." She shrugged.

"Well, look, dammit!"

She went to the window overlooking the street with the river beyond. Since her living space was on the second floor, over a parking structure below, she had a clear view of the block. There was a phone booth outside the convenience store she sometimes shopped at about a block away. But just then she saw a large black Mercedes pull up in front, and two men got out. One of them looked up at her through the window and nodded, giving a little wave.

Her blood pressure spiked as she stood at the crossroads, suddenly wanting to help the woman and not knowing what to do.

She waved back.

And then there were the sounds of footsteps coming upstairs to her front door.

"Natalia!" yelled Carmen. "Help me!"

She remembered the look on her grandmother's face when she was taken away that day. All of a sudden, it occurred to her that the woman she'd loved so much did nothing to stop her from leaving with that man who later abused her.

Sold? Was I sold like one of her canaries?

Rage boiled her blood as she recalled being raped repeatedly, her private parts bloodied and torn, her future stolen, the future of all the other women she'd been reading about stolen at her very own hands. The scars from the rapes weren't what made her ugly. It was what she had done that made her despicable. Unworthy of being loved. She was a non-person.

As she greeted the two men who wore black gloves, men she'd never met before who smiled and respectfully greeted her by her name, who'd been told perhaps the most intimate details of her life, how she'd been compromised into this position, she found it quite easy to lie to them.

"Gentlemen, she's in the bedroom. She just woke up. I'm afraid she doesn't like oatmeal."

The younger, shorter one gave her a smirk. "That's okay. We'll make sure she gets something good to eat. We'll take good care of her. You don't need to worry."

He reached into the breast pocket of his suit jacket and took out a thick envelope. Natalia saw the gun strapped to his side. He was about to present her with a lot of money, but the money didn't mean anything anymore. As her hand went forward to accept his gift, she lunged, grabbed the gun from his holster and shot him right above the bridge of his nose.

As the first man fell backward, Carmen let out a blood-curdling scream, which distracted the second one, who had begun unholstering his weapon. Natalia did as she'd read in her detective novels. She held the revolver with both hands and shot, hitting the man in the throat. He stumbled forward, trying to reach out to grab Natalia, and would have, if she hadn't backed up just enough so he fell to his knees, clutched his throat, tried to stop the blood spurting from his neck and fell on his belly. She aimed the barrel at the tiny bald spot centered at the back of his head and pulled the trigger.

CHAPTER 14

"**W**HAT THE HELL'S the matter with you, Kiley?" Corbin Newman III screamed into the phone. "We expected you back in Portland today. That's what you told Chief Rayburn, which I relied on, since you didn't have the courtesy to return my call as you promised! You promised, God dammit! And since your number was disconnected, we had no way to check in."

"That's why I'm calling, to let you know."

"You've left me in a pickle, little lady. I'm not happy about all of this. There's a very real chance the paper's going to get sued over your allegations—unsubstantiated allegations now since you couldn't be bothered with completing your investigation."

"That's not fair. You published it early." Kiley had never heard him so angry.

"Oh, fuck You! You're the one who dug up all this dirt. Problem is, I trusted you with the details. I promised the chief you'd be bringing all that in. I got the mayor all over my ass and more attorneys and other media outlets interested in me, personally, dragging Rosalie and her radio station through the mud as well, than if I'd cured Herpes or something."

"Corbin, listen to me. The facts are true. All the facts stand," she insisted.

"Really? Well, where are all those sources? You better have them all wrapped up, checked, and double checked. You better have fingerprints and blood samples because you're going to have to help defend all of us in court. These guys don't mess around. I think you're about to be arrested."

"What? That's ridiculous."

"Really? Have you talked to the chief?"

"He's going to be my next call."

"I don't know this for sure, but I think they're sending someone out to interview you, someone from the F.B.I."

"But they don't know where I am."

Kiley heard papers rustling in the background. "How does 917 Beach Access Road do for you? Is that close enough?"

That was the address of her rental bungalow. Now she saw how Jason had been right. She should have contacted the Pinellas County Sheriff's office days ago, when she first came out to Florida.

"I don't understand why all this is centered on me, Corbin. Everything I said in my articles is true. I have the tapes and the interview notes. And I can't be made to produce them, to protect my sources. But I can voluntarily turn them over to law enforcement. I want to cooperate. We're all on the same side."

"You would think so, wouldn't you? This is worse than a hornet's nest. People are going to die."

"Pardon? I don't understand."

"This morning. There's been a shooting. Two property owners were shot in their own building. One of those centers."

"Which one?"

"On Canal road, warehouse district, close to the river."

Kiley knew about the shelter but hadn't interviewed the staff yet. It was one of the places she asked Carmen to check out.

"How could I be involved in that? I'm not in Portland, Corbin."

"There were no girls there. Looks like there had been, but everyone's disappeared. If what you suspected is true, someone could be cleaning up loose ends. All those girls you thought you wanted to help are disappearing faster than my first marriage. They're scattering. We're not going to have any witnesses."

"Where did you get this information from?"

"Well, not from the mayor. He's not talking to me anymore. He told me personally he was going to see to it I paid for creating this stain on the good city of Portland and, indirectly, on him."

"So who told you the girls are disappearing?"

"Martin. He found Carmen's phone, some of her notes she'd left behind. He's been doing what he can, but honestly, Kiley, you need to be here to help direct him. You need to give us something as a cover. No one will talk to him. He got a tip from his friend at the police."

"I told you that was going to happen. So does anyone know where Carmen is?"

"That would help a lot. But no. Nobody's talking, if they know."

Newman was calming down, and with that, Kiley could finally think. At least Carmen hadn't turned up dead, although that was still a likely scenario. Kiley knew things would be unraveling quickly, and in the broad brush of sweeping everything into the trash, people's lives were at stake and their livelihoods messed with. An old reporter she met at a press dinner told her that, when a scandal brewed, the guy or gal in the white hat who came in to save the day was usually the real guilty party.

"They'll make sure everyone else pays. They'll make deals and clean up the whole thing and walk out a hero.

That's the one you have to go after. Eventually, you'll get him, but you have to be patient and persistent," he had told her. She'd never forgotten those words, which now haunted her.

That was going to be her new focus.

AS PROMISED, AND using her last burner, she called the chief. This time, he answered the call before the second ring.

"Well, well, well. Look who we got here? I'm guessing this is Kiley Worthington?"

"Yes, sir. I apologize for the change of plans. I was advised not to return to Portland, sir."

"I see. Well, I hope you have a good lawyer. He could tell you I can demand your presence here. And if you don't comply, I can have you arrested and escort you back. Whichever you prefer."

"I plan to come willingly. I am making arrangements now."

"I'm assuming you know that this is now a murder investigation?"

"My editor said two homeowners were—"

"I wouldn't exactly call them homeowners. They were on title, along with a whole group of investors. What they have here is the equivalent of a modern-day covered hopper car scheme. They launder some of their losses, and get a tax break doing it. The big difference is, they didn't lose money. They were making money. Lots of money."

"Why are you telling me all this? I thought you said I was a suspect or something."

"I know you aren't. But that doesn't mean you won't get charged with something. I'm trying to press you into service. I need your notes, your audio recordings of all your research, which I understand from your editor you have on your person."

Kiley admitted she did. There wasn't any point in not doing so.

"Why don't you go after the other owners? Maybe they were involved," she suggested.

"I'm not as quick and smart as some, but I know a who's who in the local crime scene, and these guys don't play nice. I'm the last person in the world they'd voluntarily speak with. They have a whole building of lawyers shielding them. No. I need to get the little people. The people you talked to. I want the victims in their own words. And we're in a race against time, because every one of those people you mentioned have a target on their backs, thanks to you."

"But I didn't give any names."

"Oh, they got the names, Miss Worthington. I'm the one who doesn't have the names. I need you back here ASAP before you wind up disappeared as well."

"Then I should go to the local sheriff here."

"I've already called them. You'll be hearing from them very soon. And I wouldn't try to run or hide."

Her body was drenched with sweat. Her stomach yawned. She could feel the bile collecting there, could smell fear seeping through every pore in her body. She felt just like the first day she arrived in Sunset Beach, where everywhere, every shadow, was a hiding place for someone out to get her. Now the police were out to get her too. And the one person who could protect her, or had any possibility of protecting her, was clear across the globe. But he'd also told her he couldn't get involved, or he'd lose his Trident. In a way, it was lucky he wasn't here. She was going to have to figure it out on her own.

And then just let things fall where they may.

She saw the folly in her earlier assumptions about how she could control this, could help orchestrate an investigation. Jason was right. It didn't work that way at all. She should have listened to him in the first place.

Now, it was too late.

CHAPTER 15

THE MORNING HAD been spent down by the pier. The men were broken up into four groups, monitoring the coming and going of passengers and the ship traffic. Jason's group consisted of eight men, while several others of the squad looked for places to hole up for the night under cover of darkness. Lt. Gridley and a handful of men stayed behind at the complex to monitor calls between Washington and the Stennis Carrier Group patrolling offshore several miles. Sven Tolar, former Norwegian Special Forces officer, or FSK, and now a freelance SEALs resource team member, was explaining how the port was operated, and what the SEALs should be on the lookout for.

"The harbor can take up to seven large cruise ships before they have to use the older pier a short distance away." Sven pointed to his left, where a military gunboat ominously sat.

"That's a little unusual, isn't it, Sven?" Kyle asked.

"I've seen it. They don't have their own Navy, so they have to rely on the Spanish for their defense. Generally, Madrid doesn't want to part with their hardware this far away from home, but perhaps, there's a good reason," Sven said, shrugging his shoulders. "Or, maybe they're also looking for the contraband, since we have their permission to be here."

"So it's not exactly a secret we're here?" asked T.J. Talbot.

Kelly Fielding spoke up. "Only approved through diplomatic channels. The local military police and civil guard aren't supposed to know. But I wouldn't worry about it."

She sat back and smiled, wiggling her eyebrows.

Sven leaned over and planted a kiss on her cheek. "You're scaring the Indians, Kelly."

"Watch it," murmured Danny Begay.

"My apologies, Native Americans," Sven corrected. The crowd, including Danny, chuckled.

It had been rumored that Sven and Kelly had hooked up after one of their earlier missions, a relationship that was off and on. Jason had been told it was mostly due to Kelly living in Portland with her former father-in-law, yet still going back and forth doing State Department work on a contract basis. Sven was in a similar stage in his career. It was a matter of timing,

Kyle had told him.

Sven continued, "In cases of weather or other issues, like a problem they had several years ago where a cruise ship was towed into port, having run into a fishing trawler several miles off the island, they digress. Before the transport arrived to deliver the ship back to English shipbuilders, it had to wait, tying up two berths because of how they had to secure it. All the passengers had to be disembarked for another ship, so space had to be made for that."

"I'm going to guess some captain lost their job over that one," said Jason.

"Oh, but there's more! When a huge storm arrived, the ships in port had to stay a couple of extra days until the weather cleared, and the whole area was backed up. During the storm, several cruise ships anchored a mile out to sea because there wasn't any more room and they were low on fuel. One of the passengers was thought to be having a heart attack. Unable to arouse the interest of any pilot during the storm, the captain took it upon himself to run his beautiful ship, the size of a football field, aground at the largest tourist beach on the island. They sent the passenger to the hospital, where it was determined he had heartburn."

Their group groaned.

Kyle turned to Cooper. "We heard that story, didn't we? Weren't we on that ship?"

"I think so, a year or so later," Coop agreed.

Sven continued, "The captain was tried and sent to prison in Italy, even though he did what he thought best to save the life of the man who was ill."

"So, don't have a heart attack on a cruise ship if it's not convenient to dock," someone murmured.

"Probably good advice," answered Kyle. "Although, those of you who were with us on that cruise from Italy to Brazil, when we got attacked by terrorists in these waters, know how generally lacking in real security training the crew on board these ships are."

Jason had heard the stories of how Kyle, Fredo, Cooper and others saved the ship and enlisted the passengers to help them during the takeover and eliminated most of the terrorists in the process.

"We have a full house, then, and with that Spanish cruiser, there's no more room," observed T.J. Talbot.

"You would be correct. But take a look on the horizon and tell me what you see, son," Sven said, handing T.J. his scopes.

"I'll be Goddamned. I count two, no, three ships out there," T.J. answered. "Did we know this?" He looked squarely at Kyle, who was also checking out the horizon.

Without removing his binoculars, Kyle answered him, "Nope. Sven's just demonstrating how we need to be looking all the time. All of you do." He handed his glasses to Cooper, who then passed them around so everyone could look at the white ships at sea.

"We don't know who they are yet," Sven added. "They could be all legit."

"Would they try to sneak in at night?" asked Damon.

Cooper, Kyle and T.J. laughed at that comment.

"They don't even come in on their own in broad daylight. Always use pilots, trained captains familiar with the harbor. But at night? That would be suicide," answered Sven.

Damon turned bright red and shrugged. "Just thought they'd have enough equipment to do it," he mumbled. Jason slapped him on the back.

"These puppies are not like subs. They don't maneuver very well. Think Titanic," said T.J.

"The most dangerous place for a big cruise ship is arriving in port. That's where there's wreckage, recent changes in the ocean floor due to storms or earthquakes or acts of intentional sabotage. So it's not really a dumb question at all, son."

Kyle went on to explain they were expecting a ship to arrive sometime within the next two to three days, and it was said to be carrying up to fifty women and possible other contraband, eventually destined for the U.S.

"All we know is that it will have Dutch registry,

Vanderdam Shipping, which is solely owned by the Vandershoot family."

"Dutch registry but Italian crew, right, Kyle?" Sven Tolar winked.

Kyle cracked a smile. "That's right, Sven. As usual, you have good intel."

"That slippery bastard escaped by bribing his way out before they could bring him back to Spain to face trial the last time we caught him," said Tolar.

"Yeah, and this time, he gets to be escorted by the Carrier Group and personally delivered to stand trial either in the U.S. or Spain. We've got them on standby to take the girls, too, if we need them," Kyle informed them.

Cooper shook his head and chuckled. "Did anyone think that one through? You got, what, two hundred sailors on board one of those cruisers, and they're taking on fifty young girls?"

"We're using smaller ones, Freedom-class littoral combat ships, about a hundred, give or take. We've got a couple on standby. They're faster and maneuver better close to land, should we need it," said Kyle. "They're practically brand new and have training facilities on board, so they're set up like a college dorm, if needed."

"Well, all right, then," Coop fist-bumped Kyle. "It's back-to-school night!"

"And you'll be on land, Coop, sorry to say," Kyle barked.

Kelly spoke next. "We're reaching out to the port officials, who are supposed to cooperate with some intel as to the schedule over the next few days. We have our eye on a couple ships, but so far, not certain. We've got to be ready to go when we get the call."

The team parked their vans at various points along the waterfront. Inside, they stored scuba gear, underwater explosive charges, and some light arms. But Kyle stressed the use of arms was only in an emergency. Like most of their missions of late, they were doing surgical strikes with hand-to-hand combat, using the element of surprise. This allowed them to extract safely without drawing attention to themselves.

Jason guessed they'd brought a bigger team because of the number of hostages.

Kyle's small group retired upstairs over the restaurant they'd been stationed at all afternoon. It was to be their temporary staging compound. Taking shifts, Jason offered to be first on watch.

"You got things under control back in Florida?" Kyle asked him.

"For now, yes. I hate not being in touch, though. But Kiley was going to fly back to Portland today and I talked her out of it last night."

Kyle grabbed Jason's shoulder and shook him.

"You stay focused on what we got going on here. There'll be time enough when we're done. I'm hoping this one won't take too long, so you're in luck."

"Yeah, but you know how that goes."

"I do. I do indeed." Kyle kicked out his sleep gear and passed out bottles of water. "Stay hydrated, everyone."

The air was hot and muggy. Sven had told him of the beautiful beaches on some of the other islands he'd vacationed on, but Jason knew it was never their luck to get to see the good parts of a country or people. He'd heard about guys being stationed in a concrete bunker for several weeks, spending their whole deployment playing personal video games on their cell phones and being completely out of touch back home. It was more like how decades of previous military operations had been conducted in Panama, Vietnam, and of course all those during World War II. It was only within the last twenty years that communication technology had changed so drastically. Zoom hadn't even been around ten years yet, so all the guys who served during Desert Storm didn't have any of that.

He hoped that didn't make them a bunch of yuppy warriors as he scanned the horizon and remarked at the movement of the stars now beginning to appear. The nature of his job was still the same. It was brutal, because rooting out evil was always one of the toughest things to accomplish, and always only a few could do it.

I am that man, he whispered from the Navy SEAL prayer. Kyle was right. He'd better keep his mind on the job and what he could control, not what he couldn't.

He heard Thomas whisper to him, like he was calling from inside that fucking blue urn.

You got this.

Jason sent him back a message, *Yup, I do. Remember how we loved this?*

Loved, as in used to?

I'm good with it, Thomas. You've got bigger problems. Are you a pelican or a sea turtle?

Jason heard the sound of laughter all around him. He quickly glanced up to make sure it wasn't real. And that brought on another wave of belly-laughing from Thomas. Jason mentally put the top back on the urn, and the laughter stopped immediately.

He whispered a prayer to the ocean to deliver up the soul of darkness, to make his movements swift and purposeful. To anticipate every move and be the lethal dose to send that evil soul back to the underworld. He heard the women chanting in the background, felt the firelight against his face and his tiny heart beating inside his chest as he watched the dancing and the magic displayed. His ancestors sang and danced with their gods because they spent so much time with them all alone, at sea, crossing miles and miles of uncharted waters, seeking land.

When all you had to observe was just water, the sky, and the stars at night, it was healthy to believe in the songs and dancing.

Kyle was suddenly next to him. "You okay?"

Jason didn't know what he was talking about. "Pardon?"

"You're singing."

"Oh, sorry." Jason scanned the room. Damon was nodding his head, yes. But no one else was paying attention. "I do these chants to keep myself alert."

"Well, stay with us in the here and now, Jason. No imaginary worlds."

That pissed him off. Kyle must have seen it in his face because he turned back.

"If I hear anything, I'll let you know. Christy knows how to reach me if need be. You did tell her to call Christy if something comes up, didn't you?"

"I did." The problem for Jason was that Kiley was so darned head-strong and overly confident he worried she didn't plan very well. He was going to keep that to himself.

SEVERAL HOURS WENT by. Jason was fast asleep, having been relieved by the second watch. He was awakened by the squawk of Kelly's com. She bolted upright and turned the device down, not to wake anyone else up, but it was too late.

"Come again?" she whispered.

They all listened while her eyes flashed recognition, and she gave them all the thumbs-up.

"Roger that. We'll be ready," she signed off.

She took a deep breath and flashed a smile as the other men began to repack and straighten their gear. Damon handed Jason an energy bar, which tasted marvelous.

"We've gotten confirmation from the Harbor authorities a Dutch registry cruise ship has requested a pilot at sunrise."

Jason didn't see a speck of early morning sun, but Kyle checked his watch. "We've got about one hour forty. Did they say it was only one ship?"

Kelly nodded.

Sven talked into his mic while Kyle informed the other groups. He called the carrier group from his sat phone to be on standby. He was told the mission was still a go from Washington.

The sky started turning a muddy pink color with streaks of gray here and there. There was no wind. Jason figured it was already nearly eighty degrees and the sun wasn't even showing yet.

"I got visual," Coop said.

Jason borrowed the scope and saw the white hull of a ship slicing through calm navy blue waters, leaving little wake that suddenly disappeared as the ship slowed. The pilot boat was speeding out from the harbor master's house, headed straight for it. He was surprised the ship wasn't any larger than she was.

Three blasts from one of the cruise ships jolted the morning calm, indicating she was going to leave port.

The Spanish gunboat wasn't there any longer, and a Magnum Class cruise ship was powering up, preparing to depart, it's pilot boat heading slowly toward the open sea, waiting. Very slowly the ship backed up and then turned, it's ballast tanks sending out their contents, helping it maneuver the bow until it was pointed in the opposite direction from where it started. Once the behemoth was fully engaged, it began the process of heading toward the horizon, picking up speed and swiftly passing markers until it was several lengths from the pier and approaching unobstructed open sea.

The waiting ship accepted the pilot as his pilot captain pulled away and made a wide half circle, coming back to port. Within minutes, the Dutchie began to move forward. It's sleek lines and quiet engines hardly disturbed the early morning air. Not long after, it was docked, powered down, and tied off. Jason saw a line of people along the railing, heard some announcements over a loudspeaker on the ship, and watched the two gangways move into position just before a procession of white uniforms traveled up the ramp and into the belly of the beast.

"It's the Vanderdam Orca," Kelly confirmed, her finger pressing the com in her ear.

"Okay, so listen up. We have an advanced team heading over to board her now. They're posing as an engineering crew doing quality checks in the engine room. The ship's Chief Engineer is a friendly."

"So far, so good," mumbled Coop as he adjusted the Velcro pockets in his vest, stuffed with gadgets. "I'm going to be roasting alive in this get-up."

Jason thought he looked ridiculous. With a red bandana around his neck, his mid-shin length khakis, canvas slip-ons, a long-sleeved shirt with a string of palm trees painted across his chest, and the vest, he didn't fit the picture of a tourist, a fisherman, a dock worker, or a beach bum. And he certainly didn't look like a soldier. The long-sleeved T-shirt took care of covering up all his tats.

Jason was only armed with his KA-BAR, but he suspected a couple of others would have light arms. It had been discouraged, so being one of the newer SEALs on the squad, he didn't want to push his luck.

They piled out of the building in groups of two or three and scattered, as they'd been instructed. Kelly walked with Kyle, who wore a yellow baseball cap backwards, and made an introduction to a security guard manning the gate before any of the passengers or other crew could board. They stopped approximately twenty feet from the gangway and waited.

A handful of orange-suited workmen walked past Kelly and Kyle and made their way on board. Jason stepped closer to Coop and asked, "What are they waiting for?"

"The ship has to clear customs, I'm guessing," Coop answered, focused on the activity before him.

Jason observed several Team Guys scattered all around the dock, some pressing against the fencing and a couple others sharing a cigarette. No one made eye contact with each other. A flurry of dockworkers were lining up electric carts to begin bringing provisions on board. Covered carts and refrigerated compartments waited. Two forklifts stood idly by, their operators waiting. Porters with baggage handcarts and six-passenger golf carts waited to transport passengers to shore for their excursion groups. Buses were lined up in a row in the parking lot, their drivers waiting.

At last, a blast from the ship started everyone in motion like a swarm of ants. Something was announced over the ship's loudspeaker. The white-uniformed port officials returned to the pier, briefly stopped to talk to Kelly, and then returned to their offices.

Streams of passengers began exiting the ship. Jason, Damon, T.J. and Coop were hailed by one of the golf carts and hopped aboard, where they were allowed to enter the security area, joining Kyle and Kelly. Several others of their team were allowed through on foot.

Kyle called the four of them into a huddle, passing out badges on lanyards. "I want you guys to find someone in customer service. Locate Amber Lynd. She's supposed to let us know where all the girls are. We don't want any of them leaving, just yet. Not until we can get the ship secured."

"Secured?" asked Jason.

"You remember, the advanced team?" Coop reminded him.

"I don't want you to do anything but locate them. They will probably be together, but might be on a couple of floors, in groups."

Kelly added, "Be aware they might have customers still in their rooms. And some of them will be scared to death and ready to bolt given the opportunity."

"Do you think Vandershoot is on board?" Asked T.J.

"Oh, he is. He most definitely is," said Kelly.

"Now, let's go quickly. Your passes will get you through the metal detector."

Jason panicked. "I brought my KA-BAR."

"Yeah, and I'm thinking a couple of you brought sidearms too. Kelly's going to lead you through. If her people are not guarding the machines, we wait, understood? This is either going to go very quick, very smoothly, or it will be long and drawn out. I don't want a firefight, is that clear?"

The group nodded.

"Okay, here goes. God, I hope this works. Just follow Kelly."

The group followed behind the State Department operative, who showed her Special Agent badge and was allowed to bring her group through without going through the metal detector. Their action didn't seem to raise any suspicion from the crew.

But Jason was concerned about Kyle's comment.

Once inside, the crush of passengers lined up, cascading down the stairwell and awaiting their debarkation, was difficult to maneuver through. In places, Jason had to nearly shove people aside to get past them.

"Coop and Jason, go do me proud. The rest of you, follow me. Coop, I'm going to be at the theater entrance. That's deck five."

"Roger that. So you want one of us to stay behind when we find them?"

"Yes."

"Then I need another volunteer," said Coop.

Kyle grabbed Damon and shoved him toward Jason. "And now there were three."

As Kelly and the other three SEALs headed toward the elevators, Coop, Jason and Damon took to the stairs, avoiding passengers who weren't paying attention to where they were going. A maze of handcarts and elderly people with luggage made their path more like an obstacle course. Coop checked the ship's map, mounted on a side wall.

"We have to go up two more. See here, customer service?" he pointed.

"Got it."

A cluster of confused and clamoring passengers had congregated at the long line of customer service counters, manned by uniformed hospitality crew who were trying to smile and attend to complaints and questions. Jason read the name badges and didn't find Amber anywhere. Finally, he heard Coop whistle. He was standing next to a white-blonde representative who pulled them into one of the booking offices.

"Okay, here's where they are. On the eleventh floor, at the back, that's stern." She handed them a paper sheet with the floor maps similar to the one posted. "I haven't been up there today, but yesterday, they had an armed guard posted on both sides. But there is a utility stairway where the guard can be bypassed. You enter that series of passages through the galley, the kitchen."

"All we're doing is confirming where they are. So they're all together?" Coop asked.

"I think so. I saw a couple of Vandershoot's men escorting two girls last night. I can't be certain where they are right now, but his men have suites all over the ship. It would be impossible to check all of them."

"Okay, thanks. If we have a question, how do we contact you?" Coop asked.

She passed out cards. "That's my direct extension, but do not leave a message. You can access our phone system from any floor, the white house phones. But be careful. You don't look like passengers and it could raise suspicions."

"Okay, thanks," Coop said.

"We appreciate what you're doing," Jason added.

"I hope you succeed. I have my own reasons," Amber whispered.

The trio chanced using the elevators and found them to be packed with passengers going down. When they finally caught one going up, it stopped at every floor until they came upon Deck 11.

The lights and sparkling pale peach and silver interior of the ship were beginning to annoy Jason. He felt like he was climbing around in an ice palace.

"Let's stick together until we find out if there are guards," Coop instructed.

They turned left, walked single file down the narrow hallway, past several service doors, which Coop pointed out, and then to another lobby which accessed a couple of restaurant entrances. Beyond this lobby was another long hallway, which curved slightly, revealing two uniformed crew members standing next to each other, blocking the entrance to the rooms on the other side of them.

Coop pretended to check the room numbers when the crew noticed them.

"Dammit, it's on the other side." He shrugged.

"Sorry fellas," he said. Neither of them smiled in return.

Coop crossed the lobby area to the opposite side and found the same situation. This time, they managed to turn around before being spotted.

"Damon, you stay here and monitor. We'll come get you in a bit after we report to Kyle," whispered Coop.

"No problem."

To avoid the crowds again, the two of them ran down the seven floors and found the theater entrance, which also happened to be stern. The doors were unlocked. Jason slipped inside the darkened theater behind Coop, where they found Kyle.

"Deck 11. Rooms 11204 and 11205 are probably where they start. Two guards posted on each side, and I didn't see a firearm, but I think they were packing. Looks like they have about twenty rooms total, including the insides," Coop told him.

"Good. Did Amber say anything else?"

"She said she saw a couple of the girls with Vandershoot's guys last night," Jason answered.

"And his men are all over the ship," added Coop.

"Okay, so we have them pretty much all in one location, which is great news." Kyle shook their hands. "Gents? How about a little cruising today?"

CHAPTER 16

KILEY REMEMBERED A discussion of Christy Lansdowne from Martel and Aimee. She knew it was the only thing she could do that she was one hundred percent certain was right. Everything else was just going to be by chance, dumb luck, a little magic, and hoping and praying she could pull off a return to Portland without getting herself or anyone else killed.

She'd tried calling Jason several times but knew he was probably in the middle of their operation. She decided to give up trying, to not interfere with his life any more than she already had, and just do what he'd suggested, to call Christy.

She'd made her airport reservations then called her landlady and left a message about vacating early. That left her cold. She didn't allow herself any space to grieve or feel any disappointment. She was making the motion, taking the steps she was required to make, trudging forward on the only path left open to her.

She was hoping this lockdown of her emotions would keep her from erupting and completely falling apart. It was one of the hardest things she had to do. She was convinced this was the right way to go about it, but wasn't sure she had all the skills she'd need. But she was just going to press on and not think about the consequences if things didn't turn out satisfactorily. A happy ending was too high to shoot for. She wanted an ending resulting in freedom for some, with minimal numbers of people hurt, including herself.

She told Aimee she was coming over to spend the night if the invitation still existed, and was welcomed enthusiastically. She hadn't told them yet about her return to Portland, but regardless of their opinion on the subject, her resolve was strong and nothing would break it. She'd already mentally kissed good-bye to this little cottage, the scene of so much possibility and love shared. If she could do that, walk away from all of that, she could do whatever else was required of her.

She packed enough for a couple of days, just enough to get her back home, and included the Beach Heals Everything sign that always traveled with her. She also made sure all her notes were tucked into her computer case. All the rest of her clothes, candles, and trinkets she'd purchased she left in a big box and was hoping to impose on Aimee and Andy to get them mailed to her later.

Before she picked up the phone, she walked outside on the patio and smelled the salt air and listened to the sounds of the surf pounding against the firm sand. The breeze was warm on her face. The moist air kissed her cheeks, implanting the memory she'd have forever of walking the shoreline, being a tiny speck of sand amongst the billions of other specs of sand. She'd found hope and healing here. That was going to be important to remember. She doubted she'd ever be able to bring herself to return here. But who really knew?

Kiley brought a baggie outside with her and filled it with bits of sandy shells without even selecting anything special. When she looked up at the moonlight on the ocean's undulating surface, she remembered Jason throwing the ashes of his best friend into the wind. Part of her would be left behind as well. All those wishes and fantasies scattered randomly, released forever.

Back inside, she zipped the top of the baggie closed, rolled it carefully, placed it in a paper bag, and added it to her carryon bag. She sat, took out her cell phone, and dialed.

"Hello?"

"Christy, we haven't met. I'm Kiley, a friend of Jason's. I met him here in Florida."

"Oh Jason. I love that kid," Christy said. "Kyle's told me Jason's quite fond of you. What can I do for you?"

"I'm not sure if he's told you, but I've gotten myself into a jam, and I have to return to Portland to help straighten out the mess I made of things."

"Oh, what kind of a jam?"

"Just stuff. It's way too much for me to explain right now." Kiley felt hot tears collect at the edges of her eyes. "I've hurt a lot of people. I didn't realize the consequences of my actions, and it's not right. I've exposed a lot of people to danger."

"I'm so sorry for what you're going through, but how can I help?"

"I just wanted you to tell Jason that—oh gosh, this is so hard to say."

"You sound like a sweetheart, Kiley. Wouldn't you rather tell him yourself?"

"I'm not sure I'll be given the chance to do that. Just tell Jason something I never told him myself, and I should have." The tears were really coming down now. She sniffled and wiped her cheeks.

"Are you all alone? I wish I could come over there and give you a big hug."

"I'm going over to see Aimee and Andy. They live just a few houses down from me on the beach, Sunset Beach."

"We've heard so much about it, Kiley. Such a beautiful place. Kyle's wanted to take me there, take the whole family there for a vacation some time. We all wish the two of them well and wish they hadn't decided to stay in Florida. But that's a good idea. You don't want to be alone, Kiley, not tonight."

"In the morning, I'm going back to Portland. I want you to tell Jason that I'm going to try to fix everything, take responsibility for all the damage I've caused. Just tell him that, in case—"

"In case what? Are you in some kind of danger?" Christy asked.

"He knows all about it. He won't be surprised. Tell him I wish we'd had more time."

"Listen, Kiley, you need to get over to Andy's right away. Promise me you'll do that."

"Oh, don't worry. After I hang up, that's where I'm going." She faltered. "I want you to tell him that I think I've fallen in love with him. He made it so easy for me. I mean, not at first. I thought he was a stalker or worse. But, Christy, I've never felt so loved before."

"That's the way these guys are. It isn't always easy, you know, but I've told that to many women over the years, that they will never meet anyone who will love them so thoroughly ever again. It takes a special man to do the things they do. They're the real deal, Kiley."

"Well, I'm going back to right some wrongs. Who knows, if I succeed, then maybe I'll get to tell him all these things myself."

"I hope so, Kiley. What else can I do for you?"

"You can pray."

"I will do that. And I'll pray for Jason too. I hope you guys will be able to finish all those unfinished conversations, Kiley. It's hard when they leave, but so special when they return. You'll see."

"Thank you. That means a lot."

"Why don't you go get some rest, and when I can, I'll deliver a message to Kyle for Jason on your behalf. I'll make sure he knows all about our conversation. So take good care of yourself and call back if you need anything else, okay?"

"Yes, ma'am. I will. Thank you again."

"Good night."

As she took one last look at the cottage, she wondered if she'd ever find such a special place again. She turned off all the lights, locked the front door and left the key under the mat, as was done when she arrived. She found her way back to the access road, headed toward the water, and walked alone to the glowing house Andy and Aimee were working on, her computer case and overnight bag slung over her shoulder. Even at this late hour the house looked warm and inviting.

Aimee met her at the back door, worry lines on her forehead.

"Did she call you?" Kiley asked.

"Of course she did. She was worried. What's going on, Kiley? She told me you're going back to Oregon? When did you decide this?"

"Tonight. If I stay, they're going to maybe have me arrested anyway. They have my address. The police were going to have me escorted home. It's now a murder investigation, Aimee. I've put a lot of people in danger, people I was hoping to protect. I have to go back to make it alright, if I can."

"But you promised Jason you'd stay—"

"That was before I learned people are in danger, Aimee. Two people, perhaps more, are already dead. I've got to find my colleague. I'm the reason she went missing."

"You don't know that for sure. Please, don't do this."

"I'm so tired, Aimee. I just want to crash."

"Okay, I've made a bed up for you downstairs. What time is your flight?"

"One o'clock."

"Well, I'll get you up for breakfast, but I'd like you to discuss this with Andy first. And we can get you to the airport if you still want to go."

"Thanks. I appreciate that."

Kiley let the computer bag and the canvas overnight satchel fall to the ground. Without even changing her clothes, she removed her shoes, and crawled into bed, completely exhausted. Then she remembered she still had the burner on her possession. Pulling herself out of bed, she slid the case open, removed the SIM card, and flushed it down the toilet.

Crawling back to bed, she fell asleep with the sounds of the ocean transporting her back to happier days bursting with unlimited potential and endless golden sunsets.

CHAPTER 17

DAMON AND JASON stared at each other, tasked with monitoring any traffic coming from or going to the rooms down the hall. Kyle sent Coop to join several other guys at the bridge. Jason worked hard to keep up with Kyle as he scurried up the carpeted grand stairway to the eleventh floor where Damon stood waiting. He was about to turn left, toward the bow of the ship, but Jason corrected him and sent him right.

"They're on both sides, here and here," he told Kyle.

"Stay here for a second," Kyle said and disappeared.

"What the fuck's going on?" asked Damon.

Jason had no idea. Their LPO returned and was on his sat phone.

"Yes, I can confirm four." He walked past them through the lobby area and disappeared around the corner for a private conversation. When he returned, his eyes were smiling but his lips were slammed shut in a straight line.

"You're not gonna tell us, are you?" Jason said, his voice barely audible. Damon's puzzled expression only deepened.

They followed Kyle down the other side hallway.

Kyle turned halfway to address him. "That's right. You'll see. I wasn't sure it was going to work, but we're gonna give it a go. You guys find something in there you can use, hang out in the lobby, and keep an eye on whomever comes and goes, okay?"

"Roger that," Damon whispered, shaking his head.

The service closet he'd pointed to was easy to jimmy open with Damon's handy multitool, which didn't even leave a dent or mark to let on someone had tampered with it. Best of all, Damon didn't make a sound doing it.

Inside, the small space had metal storage shelves containing cleaning supplies, soap and paper products on top, with a row of buckets and rags on the bottom shelf. Smack in the middle of the area was a rubber two-tier wheeled cart stacked with trays of dirty dishes.

Jason could see that there was a pulley system that apparently brought supplies from the kitchen and took dirty dishes, utensils, and trays back down to be cleaned. A large red button to the right of the plexiglass chute cover appeared to operate the system with an easy up or down arrow. He noted the opening was large enough to accept a child or small man, perhaps a woman inside. If the down arrow was pushed, it could give someone an escape hatch to the fourth floor and the kitchen area below.

But it would never accommodate Jason's large frame. Probably was too small for Damon even.

"I saw waiters riding one of these down from the dining room when a bunch of us took a San Diego to Mexico cruise last year."

"Seriously?" Damon whispered; his forehead wrinkled.

"Yup. He even balanced a tray over his head, held on with the other hand. But these are little guys."

"No wasted space."

"I'll bet there's a maze all over this ship the passengers never see."

Damon whistled.

"Come on, let's quickly transfer the dishes and get this cart out to the lobby like Kyle asked." As Damon began the transfer, Jason checked the hallway in both directions to make sure no one was coming. He could hear the guards just around the bend, their voices bouncing off the slick metal-paneled surfaces of the narrow hallway. He guessed their accent was either Dutch or German.

With a bucket and several rags, along with some rolls of toilet paper, they wheeled the cart to the marble-floored lobby area and began to wipe down handrails, spraying cleaner while they worked. Jason covered the stairway to the half floor while Damon worked the lobby elevator doors and beyond where a glass railing overlooked the interior lobby cathedral.

Uniformed staff passed by and didn't say a word. Several young waitresses took the elevators down, speaking in some Oriental tongue. There were no passengers coming through, so Jason guessed they were all housed in the bow where he noted the larger suites were located adjacent to the pool and private access to the gym and spa areas.

He joined Damon, looking over the glass balcony at an empty interior. Only the sounds of bottles being stacked, and glasses being stored interrupted the happy music piped in from everywhere that was giving him a headache.

Several floors down, they watched Kyle talking to a ship's officer, along with three other uniformed personnel. One of them appeared to be the captain. The two smiled warmly and shook hands then separated. Fredo and Cooper headed off with the handsome officer, while Kyle disappeared in the opposite direction, his phone to his ear.

They continued their mock cleaning until Jason felt the rumble of the ship's engines cranking up. There were sounds of shouting as something was developing at one of the lower levels. Jason ran to the side, the sliding glass doors opening to the outside deck. As they glanced down, they saw the ship actually pushing away from the pier, without the gangway and umbrella covering being removed first. Several armed guards appeared, running down the pier, until they ran into a group of Civil Guards, who had taken a reddish-haired, pink-skinned gentleman in a white suit prisoner and were leading him to a waiting police vehicle just beyond the gates.

The security detail stood down immediately and watched as the man was escorted by them in handcuffs.

"Holy shit, he's right," said Jason.

"Is that who I think it is?" asked Damon.

"Fuckin' Jens Vandershoot."

"We better get back to the hallways," barked Damon as they turned to go back to their positions. Just before they left the deck, Jason saw the gangway twisted like soft aluminum and fall into the sea.

"Did you know about this?" asked Damon.

"Fuck no. But he said something about going for a cruise today. Do you suppose everyone got on board? Now what do we do?"

"We each take a hall and don't let anyone pass," said Damon.

The two guards on Jason's side were still there, but they were rapidly speaking into a device that crackled and gave back no instructions. Doors were opening on the floor. Jason could see young women poking their heads out and being ordered to return their rooms. But panic was beginning to take over, and a small crowd had developed behind them.

Jason knew the guards were about to abandon their post and got ready to detain them. He hoped the women stayed out of his way. He surprised the first guard and quickly held his knife to the man's throat. He saw movement out of the corner of his eye as Fredo, T.J., and several others came barreling down the hallway, giving the assist, tossing the man to his knees and securing his hands with zip ties next to his encumbered teammate. Danny and Trace reassured the girls that they were safe and escorted them back to their rooms.

Jason's pulse was racing as he leaned against the wall, fumbling for the pocket to stow his knife. T.J. walked up to him and placed his hand on his shoulder, and squeezed until it hurt.

"Are we having fun yet?" T.J. said, his eyes sparkling.

Jason licked his parched lips and discovered he'd been holding his breath, so let it out and took in another. "Mother of God. Did we just steal a cruise ship, T.J.? Is that what we did?"

"Nah, we just borrowed it for a bit. We got a little rendezvous all scheduled with the U.S.S. St. Louis in about three hours. All is well. You did good, kid."

CHAPTER 18

ANDY WAS NOT happy with Kiley's decision to return to Oregon without Jason.

"You're being short-sighted, Kiley. I'd go to the sheriff here."

"And get arrested? Sent back there in handcuffs?"

"But, Kiley, the more you try to do on your own, the worse it's going to look for you," he added.

She was getting angry. "Andy, I don't think you understand. I have no options. I have to go back."

"You're relying on a couple of phone calls. These are not people I know or would put any trust or faith in. They may be good people, but, Kiley, we're talking about a murder investigation, and the possibility that you may be a huge target. It's like just walking in and saying, 'Here, take me.' That isn't smart. You're giving up."

"I am not giving up!" She stood, pushing back from the table laid out with her breakfast Aimee so lovingly arranged. A breakfast her stomach wouldn't let her touch. "Are you saying you won't take me to the airport? Because I'm going. I'll take an Uber if I have to."

"I'd rather take you to the sheriff's department, Kiley. That's where you need to be right now. You have nothing to hide. What could be the harm?"

"Because after they're done with me, maybe they won't let me leave—"

"Yeah, for good reason," Aimee inserted.

"It's for your own good," pleaded Andy.

"But what about the women I exposed? I won't get there in time to help find them. Carmen? Should I just turn my back on everyone? The paper?"

"You're not thinking straight, Kiley," whispered Aimee. She came around the table to give her a hug.

"Don't!"

Aimee backed up, her palms stretched outward. "Okay, do it your way, Kiley. We just want to make sure you stay safe. Jason would want that too. You know he would," she continued. "Christy said—"

"So my conversation's been bantered all about then. The *personal* things I said to her were revealed to you."

Andy stood, yelling, "Stop it. You're only thinking about yourself and your own guilt. What about us, Kiley? Have you even thought about what all this could do to us? You staying here has involved us, and I'm not allowed to get involved. I'd like to pass this off to the proper authorities, but you won't let me. And just like your friends back in Portland, you're going to go streaking out on your own with no consideration for anyone but yourself. You lied to them. You lied to us. Worst of all, you lied to Jason. He believed you when you told him you'd wait for him to return. Doesn't that count for anything?"

"I don't want him risking his career to help me. I got myself into this mess; I'll get myself out of it." Then she addressed Aimee. "And, my feelings don't have anything to do with it. I'm sorry I ever embroiled any of you in this."

Aimee hung her head, silver tears coursing down her cheeks. Andy placed his arm around her, sat beside her, and gave her a hug. Finally, he looked up, and asked, "At least can I make some phone calls? We've got contacts in Portland. Maybe they can help you."

"What do you mean?" Kiley asked, returning to her chair.

"One of my buddies, Tyler, he's over there with Jason right now, is from Portland. We have another Team guy, Trace, his brother-in-law, who married Tyler's wife's sister. She still lives in Portland. Tyler's parents are still there. And…"

Andy waited until Aimee looked up at him.

"Should I get him involved?" he asked her.

"Better him than putting this on the Grays or Gretchen's family."

"Through another one of our guys, there is a man there who might be of some help. He's a billionaire whose daughter we rescued last year, from pirates doing the same thing you've run into. Who knows, maybe they're all connected. Jason spoke to me about this even. I'm assuming he's talked to Kyle. But I think if it's protection you need, this Colin Riley could be of help. He'd like nothing better than to help you get these people. But at least he'd know how to keep you safe."

"What makes you think I can trust him? Some of these organized crime guys have money too. And they're connected."

Andy leaned forward on the table, reaching for Kiley's hands. He squeezed them. "He's been trying to recruit several of us from the Team to form a kind of *Posse Comitatus*."

"Now who's talking illegal, Andy?"

"I'm not doing it. Some are considering it. That's probably not the right term, but what I mean to say is he wants to create a force for good. If it can be done, he'll do it the right way." He sat back, removing his hands. "You know what they say...the enemy of my enemy is my friend? He hates those guys with a passion. He'd like nothing more than to help others now that he's got his daughter back."

Finally, Aimee agreed.

Andy placed the call to Brandy, Tucker's wife. She gave him Riley's contact information and the number for a former San Diego policeman who was starting to train to work for Riley, Bryce Tanner. Andy said that Brandy was very reluctant to give out this information.

"But she trusts me. I said it was a matter of life or death, and that you were in love with one of our guys. That was what she cared about the most, just for your information."

"Sounds like someone I should meet, if I get the chance," said Kiley.

Aimee stepped into the conversation. "You put any of this in a newspaper when all this blows over, I'll be coming for you as well." The stare she gave Kiley scorched her toes.

THE THREE OF them headed for Tampa airport in plenty of time to catch the plane. It had been arranged that Colin Riley would send a driver and a car to pick her up at the airport. She said her good-byes and promised to pick up a burner phone in one of the airport shops and give them an update when she landed.

At last, seated by herself in the only open seat she

could get, a first-class ticket that cost as much as most people's mortgage payments, she relaxed and fell asleep.

IT WAS RAINING when she touched down, which she'd totally expected. It matched the way her insides were feeling. She turned on her cell and left a voice message that she had landed and was headed to the exit outside baggage claim, which was the arranged pickup location. She asked that they forward her new number to Jason and to Mr. Riley and his team.

She decided not to call her editor until she'd had a chance to discuss her situation with Riley. She was one of the first passengers to exit. She traveled down the gangway, approaching the concourse, her computer bag and case strapped over her shoulder. It gave her no joy to be home. It really didn't feel like home.

A crowd was waiting to board the next flight. There was an airplane representative waiting just outside the entrance.

"Miss Worthington?" the attendant said. Her accent was Russian.

"Yes."

"Hi, I'm Amanda," she said, extending her hand. As they shook, the woman continued. "We've made some special arrangements for you to exit the terminal with private security for your own safety. Do you have other luggage?"

"No, this is it."

"Great. Now, if you will follow me."

Kiley started to walk behind the young woman, and then asked, "This was arranged by Mr. Riley, is that correct?"

Amanda turned and gave a nod. "Yes, ma'am. He wanted to be sure you were kept safe. It's all been arranged."

"But what happened to the driver I was to meet down by baggage claim?"

"Oh, we're working on the approach. The drivers and pickup areas have had to be moved due to the construction. We didn't want you to have to walk to the other terminal, so he'll meet you downstairs instead. Much safer." She wrinkled her nose.

Kiley was surprised Mr. Riley had agreed to come himself.

They walked through a security door and down a stairwell to a private parking lot designated for personal jet travel. Several expensive vehicles were waiting, some attended to by uniformed drivers. She appreciated not having to walk in the rain.

"Can I carry any of your luggage?" Amanda asked.

"No. Thanks. I'm fine." Kiley clutched her computer bag tight against her body and continued.

"Here we are."

A black Bentley with blackened windows sat with its motor running. Waiting to open the passenger door was the driver in uniform, including a hat and black leather gloves. He tipped his hat and reached down to take her bags.

"No thanks, I'm good."

The door was opened. She ducked to step inside the darkened interior. Before her eyes could adjust to the darkness someone had a hand over her mouth, and she smelled some sort of pine tar substance, which made her dizzy. Her legs and arms stiffened, and she collapsed on her knees inside the cab, falling on her computer bag.

No one helped her up. The door was closed behind her.

And then she passed out as the car motor revved up.

CHAPTER 19

THE U.S.S. ST. Louis was a fast ship, especially for its size, spanning over the length of a football field. It was outfitted with new equipment being used by the Navy for the first time, enabling them to track and monitor shipping lanes increasingly at risk in the Mediterranean and the north coast of Africa. The Team Guys were fascinated with the grand tour they received. But one of the things the St. Louis could not do was show up at the harbor in Las Palmas, since there was no agreement between the Navy and the local autonomous government on Gran Canaria.

The incident with the Dutch ship had already created a stir. Kyle was told all would be arrested if it returned to port, so the Vanderdam Orca was already headed back to a friendly port at Gibraltar. This meant the SEAL Team was to be transported by a small fleet of fishing boats conscripted for the mission, where they could be dropped off at various locations on the island, regrouping later.

Jason couldn't wait to let Kiley know he would be home sooner than originally thought. He was still shaking his head how quickly the mission came to a conclusion. They'd rescued thirty-seven women, most of them from Eastern Europe and Africa. They'd seized a cruise ship worth more than the entire GDP of the Canary Islands. It would be converted to conservation and humanitarian aid, possibly returned as a desperately needed hospital ship. But the whole incident would be years in the paperwork filing alone, not to mention the diplomatic issues it raised.

But Vandershoot would serve time, either in Spain or the United States, because of the flagrant nature of his offenses and government agreements to cooperate in ending human trafficking. At least, it was a start. All the men on the team were pleased, nearly celebratory.

Kyle, Coop, Tucker, Trace and several others were eating dinner with Jason and Damon, when Kyle got a call from Washington, relaying a message from Christy. He was given permission to speak with her privately.

When he returned to the group, he was silent. He didn't even laugh when Damon and Fredo imitated one of Jason's Maori chants. He'd promised to add some of his routine to their exercise program.

But when their eyes met, Jason knew something was wrong.

"You have news?" Jason started softly, fear curling

up from his belly.

"I do. You want to do this here, or you want to do it private, Jason?" was Kyle's response.

It wasn't a hard decision. These were his brothers, as dear to him as Thomas had been. He also trusted Kyle wouldn't offer him the choice if it was really bad, so he agreed.

"Kiley's been kidnapped, Jason."

This was not expected. "This happened in Florida? How are Aimee and Andy?"

"What about Martel?" asked Damon.

"Everyone in Florida is fine at the moment," said Kyle. "She went back to Portland, and they took her from the airport."

"But how could that be? She told me she was waiting to go back. I'm practically back home now. What happened?"

"There have been some murders in Portland, related to the stories she was following for the paper. I guess she got threatened by the police, and they were preparing to arrest her and bring her back anyway." Kyle leaned forward. "I'm not real happy about this, but apparently our friend Andy got in touch with someone you know very well, Kelly. Your father-in-law."

"Oh shit. He didn't," she said.

"He'd sent a car over to pick her up, but someone got to her beforehand and she never showed."

Jason had never felt so helpless. He couldn't believe she would actually be so careless with her personal safety. "I don't even know where to start, Kyle. Are the police on it? Does anyone really know anything or are we guessing here?"

"Riley's on it. He's got a former cop working on it too, to be a liaison."

"That would be Bryce," mumbled Tucker. "Wow, this is a real shitstorm. It keeps getting bigger and bigger. Now they've gotten my household involved. This is dangerous stuff."

"We need to get to her," said Jason. "Can I get released on an emergency basis?"

"And do what?" asked Kyle. "Get involved with a shootout with the local mob? A shootout with police? Take your pick, Jason. Your Trident could be at risk here. I'm not sure there's any arrows in your quiver, if you catch my drift."

"But I have to do something. You can't just make me wait here, processing paperwork, sitting on my ass wondering if—"

"Kyle, you should let Tucker, Damon, and Jason go. Get them released," Coop said.

"That your professional opinion, Coop? You gonna risk my career, too?"

"I'd do it for you, Kyle. You know I would. We'd all do it for each other."

"But for what? If I thought it would do any good, I could justify it."

Tucker pounded the table. "Fuck this. Riley's been after me to join his little venture. Maybe it's time to go do it." He turned to Kelly. "You know what he's capable of. Does he have the network, the resources to do a hostage rescue?"

"I would never underestimate Mr. Colin Riley. Those who dare do so at their own peril. He has more allies than I'll bet the police up there have. And it's what he lives for. He could do it. I don't know what he's got planned, but I think he could."

"Thanks, Kelly." Tucker stared back at Kyle. "My mind's made up. I'm all in. Those are good enough odds for me. I'm taking them, if you'll let us. Get the three of us released, and I'll do what I can to keep the youngsters from getting snagged by something awful. I saw firsthand from the look in Bryce's daughter's face what those guys can do. This has got to stop and I won't be able to live with myself unless I try."

"I'm in too. No matter what. I've gotta try," said Jason. "I don't care what it costs me. We have to stand up to this evil challenge." Jason felt the whole room was with him as well. He was grateful for the moral support.

"And you, Damon?"

"Shit, Kyle, Martel would never forgive me if I didn't try. Besides, there's no risk. She wants me to go teach school or something. There's no way she's gonna go live in San Diego. That was a pipe dream. My priorities are all changed."

"They must be putting something in the water there," Kyle said, shaking his head. "What is it?"

"It's the sunsets. And while you're at it, release me too," said Ned. "If I can't defend one of our own, what's the point? The war's come to our soil. Time to do something about it."

Kyle studied all four of them, one by one. Jason knew he was trying to sort out all the screaming going on inside his head. And if he didn't do it quickly, he was about to lose his whole squad.

"God damn it! Give me a minute." He whipped out his sat phone, got up, and headed outside the dining hall.

"What if they say no, Tucker?" Jason was worried.

"Well, we could start a mutiny here, but somehow, I don't think that will turn out as well as our cruise ship caper," answered Tucker. "It's out of our hands, kid. Sucks, but they own us. If they say no, then we stay."

They didn't have to wait long. Kyle barked at the doorway. "Come on, you four. We're cutting you loose. There's a Seahawk getting ready, with your names all over it."

In less than ten minutes from start to finish, the four SEALs boarded the brand new forty-two-million-dollar bird and were dropped off on the far side of the harbor. Lt. Gridley and two men were on their way to pick them up and escort them to the airport. They wouldn't get there for at least another twenty-four hours. But they were on their way.

CHAPTER 20

KILEY WOKE UP lying on a dirty mattress that smelled of things she didn't want to think about. Her neck was stiff, and she had a throbbing headache. Her whole left side was painful, like she'd been thrown on the mattress roughly like a piece of meat while she was unconscious.

She heard coughing and realized she wasn't alone. Opening her eyes, daylight seeped into the structure somehow. She sat up and discovered she was in a cage. Immediately, her chest began to constrict and she became woozy.

Breathe! Breathe!

Scanning the warehouse-type building, she saw more than a dozen other cages, all containing young girls. Some were sleeping on dirty mattresses like hers, but others were sitting up, their backs propped against the metal sides of the compartments. Most of their expressions held sad contemplation.

"Hello, does anyone know where we are?" she called to the room. Her words echoed ominously.

Most of the girls looked up, and a couple of them stood. One of them put her fingers to her lips and motioned for her to be quiet. Then she pointed to a roll-up doorway and a desk manned with a guard, who was hunched over, snoring.

Kiley searched the cage and discovered her purse was missing.

And so is my computer!

She felt the pocket of her jeans and was gratified to learn that the thumb drive she'd made of her computer's contents was still there.

Thank God!

She tried to get her bearings, listening to anything from outside that might give her an indication where the warehouse was located while several of the girls watched her. She heard freeway traffic, which wasn't much of a help. But then she heard the sound of a train streaking by and then quickly disappearing. It wasn't one of the long trains hauling freight but probably a passenger run.

She heard a police or ambulance siren off in the distance and then heard the sudden blast of a large vessel traveling nearby, just like the cargo ships that went in and out of the harbor along the warehouse district of Portland. There was a commuter run she'd taken many times, so she was fairly certain she knew what general area she was housed. She was within a dozen blocks of her old flat and probably had jogged past this building.

She stood and studied every cage, wondering if she'd recognize anyone. All the girls had long brown or black hair, all were very slight, young, and terrified. Most of them appeared to be either Latino or Asian. Carmen was not among them.

The sounds of a diesel vehicle of some kind came very close to the roll-up doors and then shut off. She heard several car doors slam shut.

Quickly, she looked for something she could use to protect herself. There were bottles and some shipping crates next to the wall, but nothing she would be able to reach. She did notice a crowbar someone had used to open those wooden crates. Wood shavings had spilled over the table where the box had been unpacked and had partially obscured the crowbar.

Sitting down, she examined the mattress. It was made of old ticking material and had buttons sewn into it, holding the layers together like they did in the old hotel rooms she'd seen. As the sound of men's voices became louder, she wiggled several of the buttons back and forth until she found one that was slightly loose, enough to get her fingers under it as she pulled, and it broke off in her hand. Kiley examined it closely and discovered it was made of metal. Portions of the little disc had been clipped and folded back on itself, and that's where she focused. She carefully pried several teeth of the metal back until she had a very small sharp edge no wider than a half inch across, but it was better than nothing. She tucked the disc inside her shoe, down by her toes, making sure nothing sharp would cut her own flesh if she had to walk.

The door opened, and four men stepped inside, all wearing suits and black gloves. One of them swiped across the face of the young boy who had been guarding the cages. The young man fell backwards, his metal chair scraping on the concrete floor and then skidding several feet before stopping. He scrambled to his feet, holding his nose and trying to stop the profusion of blood cascading down over his lips and onto his shirt.

Another car arrived, and a fifth man entered, dressed in a police uniform.

Kiley studied the tall lanky cop, considering whether she might have met him somewhere before. Then she recognized him as one of the men from the mayor's task force on human trafficking, a man she'd interviewed for her story. At the time, she'd thought him very helpful, but when all the leads he gave her dried up, she had wondered.

Well, the answer was right in front of her, heading across the floor between the other cages and walking deliberately in her direction. He hadn't tried to cover his face, which gave Kiley the sinking feeling he wasn't worried about her recognizing him for a very specific reason.

She'd come to the end of her tether. This was where the story was going to end. She'd be written up under Michael or Corbin's heading,

Local Investigative Reporter found Murdered in Warehouse Sting Operation.

She remembered what the old reporter had told her. It verified his story. It was always the ones who were in charge of the clean-up that were the guilty ones. Those were the ones to watch, be patient, and go back and keep drilling for more information after the scandal was sanitized.

That probably also meant her other hunch had been right. The mayor was involved up to his eyebrows. Or, at best, he was somehow compromised.

"Hello, Kiley," Officer Damien Woodhouse said, standing with his hands on his hips in front of her door. "Are they making you comfortable?"

She didn't look at him.

"You get a little rest?"

He kept digging.

"Hmmm? You always had so much to say, so many opinions, so many theories and ideas. I enjoyed your articles in the paper, although you were a pain in the ass."

She glared up at him. "Good."

Reflexively, he lunged for her through the bars, but Kiley was quick to back up out of his reach.

"I tried to warn you several times, Kiley. You just wouldn't give up. Now see what you've brought on yourself? On the reputation of the paper? Did you know that there's going to be a full retraction printed tomorrow? Too bad you won't be seeing it, though. I wrote the piece myself."

One of the suits walked over to Woodhouse. "Can you hang for a bit? We've got to pick up a package. I'll be back and we can load them up." He glanced down at Kiley. "Finish things."

"Sure, I'm fine. You leaving the kid?"

"You're his ride. I guess so."

"Okay with me. You count the inventory?"

"Sixteen."

Kiley knew that didn't include her, but she didn't dwell on that. The odds had just swung in her favor slightly. She had to find a way out of the cage first. But she had a plan.

Once the door slammed shut, she put her plan into motion.

"I guess you're too scared to let me out to go pee. Did I get that right? I should just pee all over the mattress?"

Woodhouse's eyes flared. "I'm not afraid of you," he sneered.

Kiley shrugged. "Suit yourself." She began to wet herself.

"Hey! Julio!" he called to the injured guard. "I need the keys. Quick!"

Julio came running. They both fumbled with the keys, which released the door. Officer Woodhouse pulled Kiley's hair, yanking her from the cage and sending her toward the restroom in the corner. As they neared the packing table, Kiley struggled, attempted to give him a knee to the groin, but he was quick enough to step away. Just for an instant, he lost his grip. It gave Kiley just enough time to grab the crowbar from under the shavings and swing at Woodhouse. The sharp end of the curved tip struck the officer across his cheekbones, nearly severing his nose from his face.

As he screamed, crashing to the ground, Kiley took his gun. A large pool of blood seeped from underneath his skull as his body went limp.

She had no idea how to shoot. But it was good enough to scare Julio into thinking she could.

"Unlock them all, right now, or I'll drill you."

The girls became agitated, whining and begging to be let out first. Julio danced around each of the cages until all but two were opened. They heard the sound of a vehicle outside, and all the freed girls ran in the opposite direction, toward a dark corner near the restroom. Kiley hoped she didn't have to do something to make the gun operable, like slip off a safety or cock it. She vowed that if she survived this ordeal, she'd learn how to handle a gun properly.

The door opened a crack. A woman's face peered in—someone she didn't recognize. Kiley aimed the pistol at her, and she shouted back, "No! Don't shoot!" in Eastern European accent, perhaps Russian.

But what happened next surprised her even more. From behind the woman stepped Carmen. The whole left side of her face was swollen and bright purple, but she was very much alive.

"Carmen!"

They ran to each other and hugged. Then Kiley turned on Julio, demanding, "Finish, until they all are released."

"Kiley, this is Natalia. She saved my life. She used to be one of them," Carmen said, pointing at the small crowd huddling together at the rear.

"Thank you, Natalia. I—" She remembered what the men had told Officer Woodhouse. "Oh my God, we don't have much time. They're coming back. There are four of them."

"We can take the bus," Natalia said.

"What bus?" asked Kiley.

"There's a detention bus outside," said Carmen.

"Do you know how to—"

"Yes, Kiley, I used to drive a school bus before I became a reporter. Let me check for keys. Be right back."

"Help me," she said to Natalia, who then ran for the girls and motioned for them to follow her back outside.

Julio was trying to quietly slip through the doorway, and she yelled at him, pointing the gun at his face again. "No way, Jose." She directed him over to one of the cages, grabbed his keys, and locked him inside.

She heard the diesel bus start. Natalia led the girls out through the door and up the steps into the white Department of Corrections bus.

Kiley was the last one to climb aboard.

Carmen ground the gears and the engine nearly flooded out, then lurched forward. Several of the girls screamed. Carmen swore, but then adjusted the clutch and smoothly drove them across the parking lot and out onto the street.

Kiley sat back and only then did she loosen her grip on the gun. She wondered if it was even loaded.

CHAPTER 21

WHEN JASON AND his three teammates landed in New York, all of them had messages delivered during their direct flight. The WIFI was out on the plane, so none of them were able to play the messages until they landed.

Jason's was cryptic. Kyle gave him little details, but left him Colin Riley's number so he could be filled in. Damon was on the phone with Martel. Ned was speaking to Madison, who was working at the Salty Dog, while Tucker spoke to Brandy. It was clear Brandy was getting an earful from her husband. But nothing was going to dampen Jason's mood.

He dialed Riley's number, and after a greeting, he put Kiley on the phone with him.

"Are you okay? God, Kiley, I thought we'd lost you."

"I'm fine. And better still, Carmen's fine. And did you hear?"

"Honey, I'm hearing all sorts of things. Everyone is getting clued in, trust me. I got Tucker, Ned, and Damon with me. We're about to board a plane for Portland in about a half hour."

"I'm so glad you're on U.S. soil, Jason."

He heard her struggle to breathe. He knew she was crying. He felt his own eyes begin to water as well. "I never would have forgiven myself if something had happened to you. Promise me you won't do this anymore. Please—"

"We saved sixteen girls. The mayor is going to jail, along with several from his task force. The F.B.I. is chasing bad guys from here to whatever crevice or crack they crawled out from. This time, the good guys won, Jason. I can finally say, I'm a force for good. Jason, I did it!"

"Kiley, but not again. Do you promise me?"

"I'm not going to promise you anything until you get your butt over here. Then we'll talk. And Mr. Riley here wants to have a sit down with all of you, too. I think you'd better hear what the man has to say. He wants me there as well."

Jason smacked his forehead with his palm but bit his tongue. Now that Kiley had had a taste of adventure, he could see she was hooked. The scared woman he met on the beach that day had turned into a monster.

Did they have a chance?

He heard Thomas cackling in the distance. If he were here in person, Jason knew he'd be rolling around on the sand, throwing shells or rocks or pieces of his sandwich at him.

THE BLACK LIMO picked up the four SEALs at the airport and shuttled them to a large gated estate overlooking the city of Portland. They carried their Navy-issue duffel bags over their shoulders, walking through a lush garden of blooming roses and rhododendrons. A light mist covered everything. The leaves sparkled with silver in the moonlight.

Riley's ornate front door opened, and Kiley ran to Jason's arms. The force with which she hit him nearly toppled them both. He'd planned to be stern with her, to talk some sense into her, but he found himself laughing instead.

Tucker was the first to enter the house, shaking Colin Riley's shriveled hand as he sat in his specialized wheelchair. Behind him stood Tucker's friend, Bryce. He made all the other introductions.

Jenna Riley appeared and timidly greeted the men, again thanking them for her rescue.

Riley bent to the side to look for Jason and then motioned for him to come over. With Kiley wrapped around his waist, he stepped into the foyer with all the others, and shook the man's hand. Although bound in a wheelchair, Colin Riley's bright blue eyes were those of a serious warrior.

"Thank you, sir," Jason said.

"Oh, that didn't turn out because of me. It's all her. Do you know what a special lady Kiley is?"

"Yes, sir, I think I do."

"I tried, but I nearly lost her. She pulled the whole thing off. This time, we won without any loss of life for any of the victims. I wish we could do them all that way, but—"

Kiley interrupted, "When the odds are in your favor, you win."

Colin Riley chuckled. "That's one way to put it."

They were served a platter of sandwiches and some soup, which was Riley's steady diet. The chitchat was light until Jenna excused herself.

"You've all got rooms upstairs we'll show you to. In the morning, after you've gotten some good rest, I want to have a serious discussion about what your future could look like," began Riley.

Tucker squirmed in his seat. Ned and Damon glanced at each other but didn't reveal any emotion. Finally, Tucker spoke up.

"I think I know what you're going to say, Mr. Riley. And these guys know I turned you down last year, and I'm glad I did. But I'm going to keep an open mind. And I'm sure these guys will too." He squirmed again. "I just want you to understand Brandy and I are a team. I don't do anything unless she okays it. So you're going to have to be patient with me, with all of us."

Damon and Ned nodded. Jason also agreed.

Riley flashed them a big smile. "I would expect nothing less. But for you guys, it's worth the wait. Take as long as you want. Now get some rest, and let's talk about what is possible, for all of us."

Colin Riley turned in his chair and zoomed across the marble floor like he was racing to be first.

"I don't think that guy will sleep a wink tonight," Tucker whispered.

Bryce nodded. "He's a very special man. Been good to me and my family. I'd do anything for my girls." He faced the four Team Guys. "He's the real deal, like you are. All of you."

JASON AND KILEY were led to a huge suite with a four-poster bed and tall windows overlooking the lights of Portland. Rain was slicing against the glass. Behind them, a fireplace roared. He never thought he'd ever spend the night in such luxury. Ideas buzzed around his brain. It just wasn't anything he was familiar with, so it was hard to stay grounded.

Until he touched Kiley.

"Sing to me," she said, running her finger over his lips.

"Now?"

"Yes, now. I want to see it."

"The thing, with the jumping and faces and all?"

"Yup. That thing. I want to watch you."

"Okay." He backed up, opened his eyes wide, stuck his tongue out and jumped high in the air, coming down without a sound. His elbows stuck out to the sides, palms resting on his hips. He began the Maori moves everyone teased him for.

Kiley giggled and fell back on the bed, watching him.

He cut it short to just watch her. How close he'd come to losing her forever. And here she was, waiting for him.

He climbed on the bed, taking her in his arms, feeling the heat of her body releasing to him. It was risky, but Jason decided to tell her the secret he'd learned about her.

"You know what I thought when I met you?"

"That I was crazy."

"There was a little bit of that, yes. You remind me of the women in my family. They were healers." He took her hand, brought it up to his mouth, and kissed her palm. "Your hands, they're healing hands. Did you know that? It's a form of magic in my culture. Healers are special. They keep the flame of life alive. They sing and dance."

"That's the most beautiful thing anyone has ever told me, Jason. Does that mean that I can heal you?"

"You did already. You healed me that night I took Thomas back to my ancestors. You were scared. But you healed me."

She was watching his eyes. A tiny smile erupted on her pretty face. "I think you heal all the broken parts of me as well."

"We'll have to work on that," he said as he kissed her. His hand slid up her tummy and over her breast.

"I think I'd like that. The hard part."

He grinned. "Will you make me a promise, Kiley?"

He saw she was holding her breath, expecting some kind of a soft reprimand. He had no such intention. "Will you come with me, to Hawaii? Will you marry me in the traditional way?"

Her eyes filled with tears. He kissed them away, gently, ending at her lips, while she spoke those beautiful words, "Yes, Jason. I will be your island girl, your forever girl."

He started to remove her clothes, slow and deliberate like she liked.

"Would you promise me something as well?" She traced the bands of his ancestors, as if she could read the stories he intended to tell her.

"Anything."

She arched her eyebrows. Raising her head, she whispered in his ear, "Would you teach me how to shoot a gun?"

Did you enjoy Book 4 of the Sunset SEALs? Please leave me a review. It's the best way you can show your love of a writer's works.

But **_HOLD ON!_**

Sunset SEALs, the series, continues! You've just read Book 4. Continue on this series with a re-visit to the characters Andy and Aimee Carr in Book 1. Book 5, The House At Sunset Beach, is out now. Read about Andy and Aimee's love story as it continues with the search for her brother, Logan, and Andy's new deployment with SEAL Team 4, calling on some old friends you know and love: Tucker, Armando, Fredo, T.J. and others! Get your copy of The House At Sunset Beach today by clicking on the link. Learn about the past love story of this magical house, and how it affects Andy and Aimee's future.

You might also want to read the Bone Frog Brotherhood series. This five-book series is all about Brandy and Tucker, how they fell in love, and how they've found a future together.

My other series:
SEAL Brotherhood
Band of Bachelors

Bad Boys of SEAL Team 3

(*New!*) Bone Frog Bachelor Series

All of my books are on audio for your listening pleasure. Go to my website to listen to audio snippets, order audio, print and eBooks, and download the reading order.

And so that you never miss a thing, be sure to subscribe to my Newsletter here.
authorsharonhamilton.com/newsletter

ABOUT THE AUTHOR

 NYT and USA/Today Bestselling Author Sharon Hamilton's SEAL Brotherhood series have earned her author rankings of #1 in Romantic Suspense, Military Romance and Contemporary Romance. Her other *Brotherhood* stand-alone series are: Bad Boys of SEAL Team 3, Band of Bachelors, True Blue SEALs, Nashville SEALs, Bone Frog Brotherhood, Sunset SEALs, Bone Frog Bachelor Series and SEAL Brotherhood Legacy Series. She is a contributing author to the very popular Shadow SEALs multi-author series.

Her SEALs and former SEALs have invested in two wineries, a lavender farm and a brewery in Sonoma County, which have become part of the new stories. They also have expanded to include Veteran-benefit projects on the Florida Gulf Coast, as well as projects in Africa and the Maldives. One of the SEAL wives has even launched her own women's fiction series. But old characters, as well as children of these SEAL heroes keep returning to all the newer books.

Sharon also writes sexy paranormals in two series: Golden Vampires of Tuscany and The Guardians.

A lifelong organic vegetable and flower gardener,

Sharon and her husband lived for fifty years in the Wine Country of Northern California, where many of her stories take place. Recently, they have moved to the beautiful Gulf Coast of Florida, with stories of shipwrecks, the white sugar-sand beaches of Sunset, Treasure Island and Indian Rocks Beaches.

She loves hearing from fans through her website: authorsharonhamilton.com

Find out more about Sharon, her upcoming releases, appearances and news when you sign up for Sharon's newsletter.

Facebook:
facebook.com/SharonHamiltonAuthor

Twitter:
twitter.com/sharonlhamilton

Pinterest:
pinterest.com/AuthorSharonH

Amazon:
amazon.com/Sharon-Hamilton/e/B004FQQMAC

BookBub:
bookbub.com/authors/sharon-hamilton

Youtube:
youtube.com/channel/UCDInkxXFpXp_4Vnq08ZxMBQ

Soundcloud:
soundcloud.com/sharon-hamilton-1

Sharon Hamilton's Rockin' Romance Readers:
facebook.com/groups/sealteamromance

Sharon Hamilton's Goodreads Group:
goodreads.com/group/show/199125-sharon-hamilton-readers-group

Visit Sharon's Online Store:
sharon-hamilton-author.myshopify.com

Join Sharon's Review Teams:

eBook Reviews:
sharonhamiltonassistant@gmail.com

Audio Reviews:
sharonhamiltonassistant@gmail.com

Life is one fool thing after another.
Love is two fool things after each other.

REVIEWS

"Well to say the least I was thoroughly surprise. I have read many Vampire books, from Ann Rice to Kym Grosso and few other Authors, so yes I do like Vampires, not the super scary ones from the old days, but the new ones are far more interesting far more human than one can remember. I found Honeymoon Bite a totally engrossing book, I was not able to put it down, page after page I found delight, love, understanding, well that is until the bad bad Vamp started being really bad. But seeing someone love another person so much that they would do anything to protect them, well that had me going, then well there was more and for a while I thought it was the end of a beautiful love story that spanned not only time but, spanned Italy and California. Won't divulge how it ended, but I did shed a few tears after screaming but Sharon Hamilton did not let me down, she took me on amazing trip that I loved, look forward to reading another Vampire book of hers."

"An excellent paranormal romance that was exciting, romantic, entertaining and very satisfying to read. It had me anticipating what would happen next many times over, so much so I could not put it down and even finished it up in a day. The vampires in this book were different from your average vampire, but I enjoy different variations and changes to the same old stuff. It made for a more unpredictable read and more adventurous to explore! Vampire lovers, any paranormal readers and even those who love the romance genre will enjoy Honeymoon Bite."

"This is the first non-Seal book of this author's I have read and I loved it. There is a cast-like hierarchy in this vampire community with humans at the very bottom and Golden vampires at the top. Lionel is a dark vampire who are servants of the Goldens. Phoebe is a Golden who has not decided if she will remain human or accept the turning to become a vampire. Either way she and Lionel can never be together since it is forbidden.

I enjoyed this story and I am looking forward to the next installment."

"A hauntingly romantic read. Old love lost and new love found. Family, heart, intrigue and vampires. Grabbed my attention and couldn't put down. Would definitely recommend."

PRAISE FOR THE
SEAL BROTHERHOOD SERIES

"Fans of Navy SEAL romance, I found a new author to feed your addiction. Finely written and loaded delicious with moments, Sharon Hamilton's storytelling satisfies like a thick bar of chocolate." —Marliss Melton, bestselling author of the *Team Twelve* Navy SEALs series

"Sharon Hamilton does an EXCELLENT job of fitting all the characters into a brotherhood of SEALS that may not be real but sure makes you feel that you have entered the circle and security of their world. The stories intertwine with each book before...and each book after and THAT is what makes Sharon Hamilton's SEAL Brotherhood Series so very interesting. You won't want to put down ANY of her books and they will keep you reading into the night when you should be sleeping. Start with this book...and you will not want to stop until you've read the whole series and then...you will be waiting for Sharon to write the next one." (5 Star Review)

"Kyle and Christy explode all over the pages in this first book, *[Accidental SEAL],* in a whole new series of SEALs. If the twist and turns don't get your heart jumping, then maybe the suspense will. This is a must read for those that are looking for love and adventure with a little sloppy love thrown in for good measure." (5 Star Review)

PRAISE FOR THE
BAD BOYS OF SEAL TEAM 3 SERIES

"I love reading this series! Once you start these books, you can hardly put them down. The mix of romance and suspense keeps you turning the pages one right after another! Can't wait until the next book!" (5 Star Review)

"I love all of Sharon's Seal books, but *[SEAL's Code]* may just be her best to date. Danny and Luci's journey is filled with a wonderful insight into the Native American life. It is a love story that will fill you with warmth and contentment. You will enjoy Danny's journey to become a SEAL and his reasons for it. Good job Sharon!" (5 Star Review)

PRAISE FOR THE
BAND OF BACHELORS SERIES

"*[Lucas]* was the first book in the Band of Bachelors series and it was a phenomenal start. I loved how we got to see the other SEALs we all love and we got a look at Lucas and Marcy. They had an instant attraction, and their love was very intense. This book had it all, suspense, steamy romance, humor, everything you want in a riveting, outstanding read. I can't wait to read the next book in this series." (5 Star Review)

PRAISE FOR THE
TRUE BLUE SEALS SERIES

"Keep the tissues box nearby as you read *True Blue SEALs: Zak* by Sharon Hamilton. I imagine more than I wish to that the circumstances surrounding Zak and Amy are all too real for returning military personnel and their families. Ms. Hamilton has put us right in the middle of struggles and successes that these two high school sweethearts endure. I have read several of Sharon Hamilton's military romances but will say this is the most emotionally intense of the ones that I have read. This is a well-written, realistic story with authentic characters that will have you rooting for them and proud of those who serve to keep us safe. This is an author who writes amazing stories that you love and cry with the characters. Fans of Jessica Scott and Marliss Melton will want to add Sharon Hamilton to their list of realistic military romance writers." (5 Star Review)

"Dear FATHER IN HEAVEN,

If I may respectfully say so sometimes you are a strange God. Though you love all mankind,

It seems you have special predilections too.

You seem to love those men who can stand up alone who face impossible odds, Who challenge every bully and every tyrant ~

Those men who know the heat and loneliness of Calvary. Possibly you cherish men of this stamp because you recognize the mark of your only son in them.

Since this unique group of men known as the SEALs know Calvary and suffering, teach them now the mystery of the resurrection ~ that they are indestructible, that they will live forever because of their deep faith in you.

And when they do come to heaven, may I respectfully warn you, Dear Father, they also know how to celebrate. So please be ready for them when they insert under your pearly gates.

Bless them, their devoted Families and their Country on this glorious occasion.

We ask this through the merits of your Son, Christ Jesus the Lord, Amen."

By Reverend E.J. McMalhon S.J. LCDR, CHC, USN
Awards Ceremony SEAL Team One
1975 At NAB, Coronado